The Waterfall Box

The Waterfall Box

by John Gordon

KESTREL BOOKS

KESTREL BOOKS
Published by Penguin Books Ltd
Harmondsworth, Middlesex, England

Copyright © 1978 by John Gordon

First published 1978

ISBN 0 7226 5490 1

Printed in Great Britain by
Ebenezer Baylis & Son Ltd
The Trinity Press, Worcester, and London

To
Edith and Les

I

A man looked out of a pub window and a boy walked down the centre of a street. The events happened simultaneously but they were a hundred miles apart. There was nothing to connect them, the people involved were unknown to each other, yet, like drawings on tissue placed one above the other, they intermingled.

The man, Harman, was in a village that encroached on to a vast plain at the foot of a steep slope. Far away, the boy, Bran Fenby, walked between terraced houses in a small town that sprawled like a carelessly dropped blanket over a few low hills. He was seventeen; Harman was past middle-age.

No matter which tissue overlaid the other the figure of the man gazing from the ground floor window of the pub would always come through stronger. For one thing, he was motionless, his presence growing more solid the longer he remained where he was, etching himself deep into the space he occupied, while Bran Fenby moved fitfully, uncertainly, and his surroundings changed with every step. Harman, moreover, was well satisfied, and Bran was filled with doubts about the way he had just behaved.

Money was what held Harman still. Alone in the room, he looked out into the village square. What he saw, where others would have seen houses, was money. The doorknockers were cash to him, ripe fruit to be picked, as were the old bell pulls and footscrapers. On the counter of the village shop the brass scales could be turned into gold, and behind the counter itself the stacks of drawers with thin black lettering were spilling over with profits that were invisible to everyone here but himself.

Harman was a dealer in antiques, buying up the past to sell to the present, and he had stumbled on a rich pocket of commodities. The village, because of its strange situation, cut off on three sides by a loop of canal and with a solid wall of houses on its fourth side, had been untouched for generations. There was something deliberate in this, secretive, and he congratulated himself on the perseverance which had made him follow the thinnest of threads into this hidden treasure house.

Bran Fenby shuddered. Through a narrow slot between houses he saw a cat climb a high backyard wall to crouch and blink in a thin patch of sunshine, but the sun had not yet reached the street and he was cold. The street, cut off from traffic by a row of concrete posts across its end, was empty, and he walked down the centre as though drawn into some current that moved swiftest there. But when he reached the end he paused, rested the books he carried under his arm on one of the posts, and looked back. He ought to apologize.

A girl, on the other side of the busy road, saw him hesitate. She knew him. I like his hair, the way he has it cut. And blond. He has the features for blond; squarish, not too thin. I wouldn't mind; would like, in fact. Look over here, stupid. Look.

She saw his blond head turn and she began to smile but it was wasted effort. Something in the street held his attention and he had turned back to face into it before his eyes reached her. Too bad. Typical. She shrugged.

He had been cruel to his mother. It was not her fault they lived here. He eased his books from the pillar, on the point of returning, but at that moment his father came out of the house. Bran heard him pull the door to and heard it jam, and then the double clumsy bang as he forced it shut. Even the door, swollen with damp, did not fit. His anger surged again. The place was as squalid as he had told her.

'Squalid!' He said the word aloud into the street.

Harman turned back into the room. He was a squat, square-shouldered man. His head was large and held on a short, powerful neck. His hair, cut short and shading to a fine white bristle at his ears and the nape of his neck, still had traces of black among its grey. His features were small and grouped together; a small nose that barely disturbed the outline of his head, a mouth reduced to a single necessary line, and eyes that at this moment glittered like fragments of mica in the crevices of a boulder.

He was well satisfied. The search was almost over. It had been long and devious, but now, in this place, he would find what he knew existed. The signs were right, the portents were good.

He drew in his breath and assessed the little parlour. There was enough even in this room to cover his purpose – as a dealer in antiques he could be expected to take an interest in the cast-iron crouching Punch that held open the door, the copper kettle in the empty grate, even the tin calendar on the wall or the whisky advertisement in flaking red and gold on the mirror over the mantle. They had their value and he would deal in all of them – and more, if he had to play a long game; but they were insignificant, the feeble trifles that would attract a routine greed. They were as nothing compared to the grand looting that he had come for.

He was about to thrust them all from his mind when prudence made him pause. To have a token of this room would serve a double purpose; it would confirm in the minds of the village that he was merely a buyer of small oddities, and for himself it would set his mark upon the place.

On the table at his side there was a little domed bell with a button. He let his fingers touch its splayed feet and then its silvery hump. This he would take with him. It would rest on a shelf within his own premises, the symbol of a true shopkeeper. He allowed himself a thin, lipless smile and struck the plunger.

Bran heard his mother's voice again, angry and hurt: 'We can't help living here. We can't afford anything else.'

Then himself: 'No. I suppose not. It's where we belong.'

He had intended cruelty and had succeeded. It sickened him. He had lingered, hoping she would give him a chance to make amends, but she had fallen silent and let him leave without a sign of any kind. His own cruelty had bitten into him. And again, now.

A twinge of pain crossed his face and he knew it. He glanced quickly around to see if he had been observed and caught the girl looking at him. She saw his good looks blur with a childish petulance and he pretended not to see her. You never knew where you were with him. Let him go. She presented her back to him and walked on.

*

The bell chimed and Harman waited for the sound to reach the ears of someone in the back rooms of the Black Swan. With this little deal out of the way he would climb the hill behind the village to negotiate for bigger things.

'I would 'a sent my boy but he's lumping crates from the barge.' The landlord stood in the open door. 'That's where I been.' He was a large man, and the dirty blue T-shirt stretched tightly across his chest was wrinkled at his armpits like an outer skin. 'Stupid bloody business when you got to have beer delivered by barge.' The small brown eyes in the big, sweating face were angry.

Harman's car was parked beyond the row of tall old houses opposite. He had discovered, and it had pleased him, that there was no road into the village square. 'At least it is quiet,' he said. 'No traffic. Peaceful.'

'But they can't get a dray through with my beer.' The landlord, wiping his large hands on a bar towel, stood just outside the door, a man interrupted in his work and not pleased about it.

Harman took the hint. 'I shall be leaving as soon as I have made my call. Would you see my case is taken to my car?'

'My boy'll do it.'

Harman inclined his head. Even in the dimness of the room his eyes had the ability to pick up what light there was and give off a yellow metallic glint. 'There's just one more thing,' he said.

The landlord wiped his hands and waited.

'This bell. I have taken a fancy to it.'

'It was give me by a friend.'

Harman recognized the lie which was intended to push up the price, and the hairline of his mouth extended imperceptibly in the hint of a smile. 'I'll give you a good price.'

'Well, I don't know.'

'It can't be of much use to you. You told me yourself; no cars, no trade.'

'I do all right.'

'No doubt, no doubt.' The business-like harshness of Harman's voice sharpened and he made a mistake. 'I'm short of time, Griffiths. Name your price.'

The landlord's voice became sullen. 'It was give me,' he said.

'You've already said that. How much?'

An angry pallor at Harman's impatience had crept in beneath the redness of the landlord's face. He said nothing.

'Come on, Griffiths. Name your price.'

'It ain't for sale.'

'It has a price. An object like this has a price.'

'How much do a "mister" cost, Mister Harman?'

For a moment Harman was frozen, then the gleam of his eyes and the crevice of his mouth both intensified. 'I see.' He was smiling. He understood his offence and could correct it. 'So pride also has a price, Mr Griffiths.'

'But mine ain't for sale. Nor that ain't neither.' He took a step forward and lifted the bell from the table.

Bran saw his father approach. The go-between. He would smile; there would be a gentle lecture; harmony would be restored. In this squalid street. Bran snatched up his books and turned away.

Harman advanced and the landlord drew back to let him pass. Neither said a word, and Harman took his grey hat from the peg in the corridor and went out into the sunshine of the square.

2

It was a picture that had drawn Harman to the village; the last clue in a long search. He could afford to allow the landlord his petty triumph, and he smiled as he stepped out into the sun.

He was observed. In the centre of the square a little grove of trees, planted almost in a circle, held up a green canopy against the sun, and from its shade a girl with careful blue eyes was watching him. She saw the sun glint from the black silk band of his grey hat, and beneath the brim she could see that the face was square but at this distance it was almost featureless, like a rock with scratch marks for eyes, nostrils and mouth. He moved with a kind of stiff smoothness that put hardly a crease in his grey suit. She shifted slightly on the edge of the stone trough where she sat and kept him in view as his small, precise steps took him beyond her towards the pillars of the hall at the far end of the square.

The picture was here. Harman let its image float in his mind. The fools could not know what they possessed or they would never have put it on view, much less allowed it to be reproduced. But there it had been on the glossy page in the publication for connoisseurs that he read in the course of his trade; its message so plain that even his self-control was broken and his first reaction had been to shut the magazine and hide it as though he was a boy with an obscene photograph. But then, calmer, he had turned back to the page. Only those who knew could read. Only an adept could see the signs.

He reached the corner and stopped to look back. A remarkable place. Terraces of rather fine, square-fronted buildings on both sides, and at the far end a little quayside and a broad flight of steps leading down to the canal. Near him a hall, perhaps a village hall, but grandiloquent enough with its pillars and frowning pediment for a small town.

The little grove in the centre was like an ornamental plot in a rich man's garden. The whole place was subtly out of scale; someone's private distortion. And undiscovered. No cars; no trade.

He turned and went up the shallow flight of steps between the pillars.

The girl was still watching when, after two minutes, he reappeared, gliding in his peculiar, sedate manner down the steps to disappear into the narrow alley at the side of the building.

She looked towards the Black Swan as though she was expecting someone, but nothing stirred and after a moment she stood up, briefly smoothed her blue dress, pushed strands of her long black hair behind her ears and sauntered along the square to pause for a moment at the corner before she also vanished into the alley.

It was a narrow space blocked at the far end by a wall, but jutting out into it was the side entrance to the hall, like a miniature wing, with pillars and a portico and steps leading up to tall doors. It was large enough to have windows at its sides but, although he must be in there, she could see nothing moving.

She hesitated, but after a moment moved forward. One half of the tall double doors stood open. Inside was a lobby, its floor covered with a large door mat, and beyond this were glass swing doors into the vestibule itself.

She climbed the three steps. The man was the other side of the glass doors. He had his back to her and had removed his hat so that he could tilt his head to look upwards at the wall facing him.

The picture was very large and hung over the door into the hall itself. She was already familiar with it but, because he stood motionless, studying it carefully, blocking her view of everything else, she was forced to do the same.

It was a portrait, or so she had been told, but it was a strange one. At the centre of it an old man sat at a table. He gave the impression of being sad and gentle, although the girl was not sure about this because his mouth was hidden by a white beard and she had learned that many a trick of character was revealed in a mouth – his lips may have been cruel. He was bald and wore a robe that hid his figure and, while it made him imposing, made it impossible to tell whether he was a large or small man. She had special knowledge, however. Her friend who lived on the hill, and she should know, had told her he had been small.

The grey man did not move, and the girl found herself trying to read the inscription on the gilt frame. It was just possible : Silas Waterfall, potter.

That was all it said, but the simplicity was false and she did not need her friend on the hill to tell her that. Silas Waterfall had done much more than make pottery. It was he who had decided the shape of the village, built the houses, given work to its people. His influence was everywhere even now. The girl grimaced slightly. The flowing brush strokes of the beard must have disguised something, just as the robes did.

The man in front of her moved and she held her

breath. She had as much right as he to be there but the longer she stood where she was the more difficult it became to appear natural. She was on the point of opening the door when, without turning round, he walked away from her across the room to where a glass display cabinet stood beneath the picture. It was awkwardly placed, blocking the door into the main part of the building, but the whole of the Potter Waterfall museum was slightly makeshift.

The man was motionless again, the bristly grey head bowed this time to gaze at the objects on the shelves within the cabinet. From where the girl stood he also was behind glass and was as still as an exhibit himself. And the chain of glass cases, things contained within things, went even further. She raised her eyes to the picture.

Potter Waterfall sat in a chair that was like a throne, and it was set on what could have been the stone floor of a cellar except that part of the back wall had been broken away to show a fragment of distant landscape. Closer, within the space of the cellar itself, there were the furnace mouths of his kilns, and along the walls, displayed with an emphasis that almost equalled the importance of the old man's face itself, were the tools of his craft. Mortars and pestles, measuring devices, compasses, dividers, pots, jars and charts. An owl roosted in one dark corner, perched on what appeared to be the skull of a horse. Closer still, on the table at the old man's side, there were bottles of coloured liquids, a retort over a spirit burner put up a plume of steam, and his arm rested against a floridly carved little casket. He was contemplating a small pottery bottle, a phial, he held on his open palm.

The girl let her eyes slide from the picture to the room. The pots and jars, the compasses, the retort, were there, inside the glass cabinet, self-consciously, almost sheepishly, displayed. Harman's grey head tilted, connecting item to item. There was a quick jerkiness in his movements, an excitement she had not seen before. As though some chemical reaction had begun, he was becoming unpredictable. In a moment he would turn round, and now that she had been a witness of something so intensely private she no longer wished to be seen.

She retreated slowly and silently down the steps and began to walk away. The excitement he had displayed gave her a feeling of superiority. The picture revealed much, but there were things a stranger would never know – things that even she had only had hints of. Her friend who lived on the hill, Sandy, knew more because the picture belonged to her family – but she was secretive about it, letting out only dribs and drabs of information. If she had told Stella so little, there was no chance of an outsider getting to know even that much. It was a family affair that only a friend would ever be told – and Stella doubted how much Sandy herself knew; even if there was much to be learned. Sandy's temperament often led her to make mysteries where none existed.

Stella glanced once over her shoulder to make sure she was not observed from the side window of the vestibule, and vanished into the sunshine of the square.

3

'I didn't trust him,' said Martha Ramsey.

'He was a sweet little man,' said her daughter.

'But I didn't like him, Alexandra.'

Her daughter sighed. 'Sandy,' she said. 'I can't bear being called Alexandra.'

'Sandy if you must. But I *couldn't* like him. Why can't you keep to the name you were born with?'

'I wasn't born with it. You stuck it on me. He had such white bristly hair on his neck it made you want to stroke it.'

Her father laughed but her mother's round, schoolgirl face remained worried. 'But I didn't trust him, Sandy.' She grimaced as she spoke the alien word; another victory for her daughter's wilfulness. She wondered where it all would end. 'I didn't trust him,' she repeated.

'Neither did I, but he was so clean you felt you wanted to put fingermarks on him. Lovely.'

Martha Ramsey sighed. She was small, dark and pretty and wore, in honour of the recent visitor they were discussing, a long brown dress with a shallow frill at neck and cuffs. Sandy regarded her. The little frills emphasized the plump smoothness of her skin, but it had all been wasted on the visitor; he would have noticed the dress no more than the loose covers on the deep armchairs in the long room. Her father was embedded in one of these, his long legs angled out over the carpet.

She herself sat on the broad window-ledge with the sun on her back. The garden sloped steeply away beneath her, disappearing into the thick forest of the hillside which had only recently swallowed the grey back of the man on his way down to the village.

'Oh dear!' said her mother.

'You're wringing your hands, Martha.' Richard Ramsey eased his long bones upright in the chair.

'I can't help it. He's got me on edge.'

Richard turned his face to his daughter. 'Your mother can't bear to dislike anyone. It worries her that there should be unpleasant people in the world.' His long face was deeply creased as he smiled and the jutting eyebrows went up and down once like the wingbeat of a small grey bird.

'You're the same,' said Sandy. 'You'd do anything to make people like you. But that little grey man wouldn't bother, and that's what I admired. It was a change.'

The eyebrows did another slow wingbeat and then he cranked himself out of his chair and stood up close to his wife. 'Our daughter sees right through us, Martha.'

'Right through you, you mean.' She gave an impatient jerk of her shoulders that effectively prevented him putting his arm around her but then relented and reached up to button down the flap of his shirt pocket. 'Just look at you. Is this the way to receive a visitor?'

'Domestic bliss,' said Sandy.

'Necessary to a man.' Her father smiled towards her but she knew he could not see her face against the glare of the sun at her back. Typical of him to be kindly without expectation of any return; she gave in to the temptation to repay his kindness with cruelty.

'Some men,' she said, 'can look after themselves.'

He smiled and was about to answer, but Martha said, 'Ignore her. You know what she's liable to say when she's in this mood. I wish you would wear something different sometimes.'

He had jeans, thick-soled shoes and a blue denim shirt with sleeves rolled to the elbows. All his clothes were well worn and patchily faded.

'I'm a working potter,' he said, 'and that's what the man came to see me about.'

'Did he indeed?' She allowed her doubt to show.

'Certainly, Martha. He put in a large order.'

'That may be.'

'I don't understand you, Martha.'

'He's an antique dealer, Richard. He doesn't want new things.'

'He has a shop. He doesn't only sell antiques.'

Martha Ramsey fell silent and, from her seat on the window-ledge, Sandy leant forward slightly. She had her father's wide mouth but not his long, slender face. In this she was more like her mother, but above the round cheeks her eyes were blue-grey and, instead of her mother's darkness, her hair was a light copper colour. Her lips and hair glistened as she watched. She guessed there was more to come.

'I don't quite see what bothers you, Martha. He's only going to get from us what he ordered.'

Her father, even though he was on the defensive, spoke calmly, protectively, and Sandy could see her mother struggling not to hurt him.

'Of course, Richard. It means work for all the people down there. It's just what we need.'

'Yes, my dear.' The eyebrows went up and came down so that his blue eyes were regarding her from beneath a frown. But at the same time he was smiling. 'Except that we've got enough work for quite a while;

20

and we don't need his order; and he doesn't want our pots.'

She looked quickly up at him and her mouth opened.

'It was a smokescreen,' he said.

'Richard.' She bit her lip. 'Do you mean to tell me you knew all the time that he was after something?'

'Not all the time. Not until I watched the way you spoke to him. Then I saw. You opened my eyes, as usual.' He paused. 'It's the picture he's after, isn't it?'

'I think so.' She looked at him for a long moment. 'But what I can't understand is why he didn't come out in the open and say he wanted it.'

'A devious mind, my dear. And the fact that it's on public display must make him wonder which way the land lies – he doesn't know if it's ours any longer.'

Sandy broke in. 'But it still is, isn't it? We've only loaned it to the village.'

'And I wish we hadn't,' said her mother. 'Then nobody would have known anything about it and we wouldn't have been pestered by horrid little men with greedy, grasping minds and voices.'

'Nice little men with pots of money,' said Sandy. 'How much do you think he'd give?'

'So speaks your daughter.' Richard Ramsey turned to his wife, smiling.

She was shaking her head, her anxiety still strong. 'Do you think he knows anything else, Richard?'

'How can he, my dear?'

'You said yourself the picture has all sorts of clues.'

'Only for those able to read them. He hardly seems the type.'

'But suppose he is, Richard? And you're always so open with people you could easily give away more than you thought.'

'And if I did, would it do any harm?'

Her eyes dropped. 'It might do. You never know. And don't forget Alice is in this as well. You did mention her when you were talking to him, and I didn't want you to.'

'Your sister is a capable woman, Martha. She can look after herself.'

Sandy had been biting her lip trying not to interrupt, but now her curiosity was too much to hold back. 'What's all this about?' she said. 'What has Aunt Alice got to do with that picture?'

For a long moment neither of her parents spoke.

'Well?' she demanded.

Her father turned towards her. 'It's to do with Potter Waterfall.'

'I might have guessed.' She had always been bored by the old man in the picture, the potter who had founded her father's business.

'He was much more than just a potter.'

'I know. I know.' In order to cut short what she knew must follow, she added, 'He did a lot of experiments and stuff trying to turn lead into gold. He was a whatsit.'

Her father smiled. 'An alchemist, and he tried to turn base metal into gold, but that's only part of it, the least interesting part.'

'Tell me more.' Sandy was sarcastic.

'He was as much interested in purifying his soul, as turning other metals into gold. In fact he did not believe you could do one without the other. All true alchemists believed that – it was never just a question of finding the Philosopher's Stone and the Alcahest.'

'The Alca-what? You've never told me about that, or that stone.'

Her father was patient. 'The Philosopher's Stone

was the chemical that would bring about the change in the base metal, and the Alcahest was the universal solvent which first of all melted everything down and made it possible. That's what he was seeking.'

'Did he find them?'

'Of course not. But it was people like him who began chemistry; they discovered things that had never been known before.'

'Did he discover anything?'

'No.' Her father shook his head.

'Pity,' said Sandy. 'We could have been rich.'

Martha Ramsey began to move towards the door, ending the conversation. 'You're well enough off, my girl. A lot better than I was at your age.'

Sandy sighed elaborately. 'We all know about that,' she said, drawing in her breath. 'You were only a little village girl until the handsome young man in the house on the hill looked down and saw you.'

'Nobody can ever say I've forgotten where I came from.' Martha Ramsey had coloured. 'I never deny it.'

'Nobody said you did,' said Sandy. There was nothing snobbish in her mother; nobody could even accuse her of it. But there was still, after all these years, a great uncertainty in her about where she belonged in the village and it was this that Sandy could not resist prodding. 'You belong up here.'

'And down there.'

Sandy shrugged. They were getting away from the point and she was just about to bring them back to it when her father spoke for her. 'Martha's got more right to things in that picture than I have,' he said.

It was his usual response, insisting that nothing was his, that they owned everything in common. Normally his wife would pay little attention, but this time she stopped before she reached the door and looked at him sharply.

'Well it's true, Martha. All those things in the picture that we've put on display could be found in any potter's workshop. The really interesting things belong to you and Alice.'

Something in what he said made her dark eyes fill with resentment, but she was silent.

'Martha,' he said, reasoning with her. 'I told him nothing. You know that; you were there.'

'You hinted.'

He raised his shoulders and spread his hands. 'It still doesn't matter – he'll never find out.'

Sandy, exasperated beyond endurance, broke in. 'Find out what?'

Her mother and father exchanged glances without speaking, and it was plain they had revealed more than they had intended. Sandy waited.

The long room was surprisingly light. The sun streamed to the carpet at her feet, and at the far end a green glimmer came through foliage clustered around another window. There was a dining table with chairs around it, but closer to her there was a scatter of deep chairs near a wide fireplace. Most of the walls were lined with bookcases and their heavy, dark wood seemed to store warmth and it was never cold in here.

After a long moment her father moved to a bureau almost hidden between a pair of bookcases, lowered the flap, took a key from the pocket of his jeans and unlocked an inner drawer.

'You cheat!' said Sandy. 'You always told me that key had been lost and there was nothing in there.'

'Some things have got to be kept from little fingers,' he said. He came back to where her mother stood near the round table and made as if to give her whatever it was he held in his hand, but she drew back, refusing to take it and he put it carefully down on the polished surface.

Sandy left her place in the sun and moved closer. Resting on the table was a small, buff-coloured flask. It lay on its side because its base was pointed, but at its shoulders there were two lugs by which it could be hung upright. It was ribbed and grooved and had a slender neck which was sealed with what appeared to be black wax.

Sandy put out a hand to pick it up but her mother drew in her breath so sharply that she hesitated.

'You recognize it?' said her father.

Sandy shook her head. She had never seen it before.

'In the picture? In Potter Waterfall's hand?'

Then she knew it. 'But why isn't it on show with the other things?'

'It's your mother's,' he said. 'It's been in her family for generations.'

'How come?' Sandy turned to her mother. 'You're not related to him, are you?'

Martha shook her head, leaving all the talking to her husband.

'Potter Waterfall was an old bachelor,' he said. 'He had no children. But your mother's family had always been housekeepers for him and when he died they were the only people close to him he could trust. So he gave them his most valuable possessions.' He picked up the little flask.

'That?' said Sandy, not believing him.

'There's the box as well, Richard.' Her mother was forcing him to tell all. 'Don't forget that.'

'Sandy,' he said, 'you remember in the picture there's a little carved casket on the table?' She moved her head slowly, recalling the painting. 'That casket also exists. It belongs to your Aunt Alice and this flask fits inside it. They should, by rights, be kept together.'

'But it was all we had when mother died. Don't forget that, Richard.' Martha Ramsey had her hands clenched under her chin. 'I wish Alice had kept them both. I wanted her to have them, but she said I had to have my share. She insisted.'

'She's a good sister to you,' said her husband.

'I know.' Martha was close to tears. 'And she's got so much less than I have. I still wish she had kept everything.'

The revelation had been disappointing to Sandy. 'Well it doesn't look much,' she said. 'What makes it so valuable?'

Neither her mother nor father answered, but suddenly her mind raced to a conclusion and she became excited. 'I know what it is – it's the stuff that makes gold!' And then her interest slumped again as she saw the impossibility. 'Or perhaps old Potter Waterfall thought it was the right stuff, and I suppose that makes it valuable in a way.'

Her father was amused. 'Potter Waterfall was a potter before he was an alchemist. He knew where true value lay. I know what's in this phial and it's nothing more – and nothing less, mark you – than the secret of the Waterfall Glaze.'

'Oh.' Sandy let her disappointment show. The Waterfall Glaze was the greenish sheen her father's pottery was noted for; infinitely boring.

'The secret of that,' said her father, 'was thought to have died with him. The cousins who took over searched high and low but they could never find anything.'

'And then, after many generations, along came you,' said Sandy, once again determined to cut his story short.

'But I had to invent it all again,' he said. 'As you know.'

'Yes,' said Sandy.

He took the hint. 'So we won't go into that.' He picked up the phial. 'I didn't know about this until after I'd married your mother.' He was laughing and he shook the little bottle, listening to the liquid inside. 'Just think of the trouble it would have saved me.'

Martha felt foolish and could not meet his eye. 'We were always told to keep it secret,' she said. 'We didn't know what it was.'

There was silence in the long room. The greenish window opened into a conservatory at the back of the house, and the scent of the flowers seemed to creep towards them.

'It's a good story, isn't it?' The eyebrows fluttered and Sandy nodded. 'But I can't persuade your mother to let me tell it.'

'You told it just now to that horrid little man.' His wife was resentful.

'Hinted, Martha. Only hinted. And he already seemed to know a good deal before he got here.'

'How could he?'

Richard Ramsey smiled ruefully. 'There are still believers in alchemy. There's a large literature. He could have picked up a clue here and there.'

'Well, if he wants it so badly why don't you sell? Make him pay a lot for it.' Sandy reached and took the phial from her father's hand. 'Although I can't really believe anybody would pay much for this.' Then she broke off, frowning.

'What's wrong?' Her mother was suddenly anxious.

'Nothing. I just thought it felt warm.'

'Give it back to your father.'

'But it *is* warm.'

'Give it back to him, for goodness' sake.'

Her father reached and took it. 'It's been in my hot hands, don't forget.'

'Put it away,' said her mother. 'I've had enough of it.'

Her father went towards the bureau. Sandy glanced at her mother. All of Martha's attention was centred on getting the bottle out of sight, and Sandy knew her moods. Once locked away, it would be a long time before the bottle was mentioned again. She had to act quickly or her curiosity would never be satisfied.

Her father opened the drawer.

Sandy, as though she was barely interested, half turned away. 'That's the first place a burglar would look,' she said.

Her father grinned. 'There are no burglars in the village.'

'Maybe.' She turned completely away to look out of the window. 'But other people know about it now.'

She spoke to her father but the words were intended to disturb her mother. She succeeded.

'Richard, that isn't really safe.'

He hesitated. It was all Sandy needed. She went over and took the phial from him.

'I know a place,' she said. 'Nobody knows about it. Come on, I'll show you.'

She crossed to the door and went out into the hall, turning to go quickly towards the back of the house.

'Alexandra!'

Her mother tried to call her back but she did not reply and did not pause. She was not going to have the little phial locked away again; she wanted it somewhere she could get at it.

4

A year. Precisely a year left of this. Bran looked down at the books on the small table in front of him. At least this would end; homework in the bedroom. One more year and then finish. Out and away for good. University perhaps. If not that, anything.

But still a year. It was a vast translucent cube in the top of which grey clouds drifted and on the floor of which he was condemned to wander. One of its walls was an exit but he did not know which. Shapes glimmered beyond them but whenever he tried to focus they vanished. There may be green fields and sunshine out there, or ash. But it would be away from this.

He pulled the table closer and the rickety leg stuttered across the floor. Beyond the foot of his bed there was just space in the window alcove for the table and chair, and he sat half-surrounded by glass like a pilot in the nose of some gigantic plane with the street stretching huge grey wings to left and right. When the anguish to get free was on him he could make it tilt, tearing it a fraction from the earth, making it lift. But after a moment the dingy house at his back would claim him and nothing had altered.

He shifted the table an inch so that it was dead square with the window ledge. The noise mingled with a sound below. The front door was opening. He waited to see if it was his mother or father who would emerge on to the pavement below, but nobody came and he leant forward to look down into the garden patch. He was a fraction too late. The door thudded once and thudded again. Someone had been let in.

He listened. Even from up here, unable to distinguish the words, he could tell that his mother was being polite. There was another voice, not loud but with a steady intonation against which her words broke and fell away. The usual deference with strangers.

The man was shown into the room directly below him. It would not be a salesman; she would not have let him in. And a friend, anybody they knew, would not have been likely to come to the front door. Bran felt his jaw tighten. A doctor. It sounded like a doctor's arrival, the quiet voices and the mumbled, unheard words. She had hoarded an illness; kept it secret. His stomach was flat and chill.

Then there were quick footsteps as she hurried along the passage to the back of the house. He listened to her scurry, and after a long moment she returned and he could hear his father with her. The door to the room opened in a burst of voices, closed gently, and the voices dwindled to almost complete silence. Bran found breathing difficult, as though the silence was a pad over his mouth, and suddenly he was across the room seeking air.

The short landing and steep stairs were a wedge of darkness, the only light coming from a little pane of glass above the front door. The voices were a solemn mutter interrupted by short spells of deathly quietness. He went down, moving slowly, as though descending into some bleak pit for a dare.

'There is no need to be nervous, Mrs Fenby.'

The stranger's voice was as precise as a surgeon's

knife. Bran heard his mother murmur beneath it. His father was silent.

'If there should be anything, Mrs Fenby, there would be no question of anybody else getting to know. I would do no more than make an examination. You have my word.'

The tiny hall was a cell. He was cold. For long seconds he heard nothing.

Then his father's voice. 'It is up to you, my dear.'

He knew that she was sitting at one end of the settee, not leaning back, but forward over her knees, plucking at a handkerchief or the seam of her skirt.

She spoke hesitantly. 'You've seen Martha, you say?'

'Mrs Ramsey was very helpful,' the stranger replied.

'What did she say?'

'She was modest, Mrs Fenby. Rather shy, as you are.' The voice was clipped, metallic and whatever sentiment it carried was consciously assumed, like a coat of paint. Now it bore a tinge of amused compliance. 'I was given to understand that she preferred me to speak to you.'

Not a doctor; it could not be a doctor. Bran relaxed. He let his head droop and his lungs fill.

His mother was speaking again. 'I don't know what to say. She hasn't been in touch, you see.'

There was a thin, rasping chuckle and the stranger spoke to his father. 'They are true sisters, Mr Fenby. Very much alike.'

In his mind's eye Bran could see his father smile, the short grey hair moving like a close-fitting cap as the many wrinkles in his face tautened.

'They were always close.' As always, his father agreed with whatever was said by a guest in his own house. 'Very close.'

31

But there were few visits; it was years since Bran had seen his Aunt Martha.

'Somewhat secretive, too?' The chuckle again.

'It would take a wiser man than me to know all that goes on in a woman's head,' said his father.

This was grovelling. Bran shut his eyes. When the voice resumed he could tell that his father was out of it now, pushed to one side.

'I learned much I did not know from your older sister, Mrs Fenby, but I also remain in ignorance of a great deal.'

Older sister. It was the crudest flattery. His mother's hair was streaked with grey and anyone who had seen Martha must have known she was the younger sister.

'I'm older,' she said. 'A lot.' She was curt, and Bran felt a pang of admiration. She would not now be huddled over her knees.

'Really, Mrs Fenby?'

'Yes, really.'

The stranger was astute and recognized a warning. He wasted no more time on compliments. 'I was given to understand, Mrs Fenby, that you may have a relic from the old days of the pottery.'

'She said so?'

The stranger evaded a direct answer. 'That remarkable portrait of Silas Waterfall, which I am sure is known to you, contains many objects which existed in his time and most of which have been traced. One or two, however, remain to be found.'

'How do you know this?'

'Your brother-in-law, Mrs Fenby, has put on an admirable display in the village.'

'I know nothing about that,' she said, and the gulf between her and her sister, between the village and the town, between money and the lack of it, was in her tone.

'The Potter Waterfall portrait is on show.' The voice strove to be tactful. 'Your brother-in-law has given it to the village.'

'That's typical of Richard.' Bran winced as his father broke in, wrecking the barrier his wife was erecting. 'You remember the portrait, Alice? It's very old; must be worth a bit.'

'Indeed it is,' said the stranger.

'And Richard gives it away.' Mr Fenby laughed. 'Money doesn't seem to matter to him.'

Bran closed his eyes. Did he have to behave like a pauper?

'Which is why I am here, Mr Fenby.' The voice, as the head from which it came faced a new direction, came through the door harsh and clear. 'The money – that is to say, the objects of value, are not all in his hands.'

There was a pause. The two men would be looking at each other. Bran could see his father's half-smile of politeness as he waited.

'Mr Fenby.' The gaze, like the voice, would be intense, forceful. 'There is one object in particular that has not yet been discovered.'

'Well I don't know what brings you here.'

It was his mother's voice, but she was politely contradicted, with a humour that was intended to flatter. And still the man spoke to his father.

'We are not always aware of the value of familiar objects. Isn't that so?'

His father laughed.

'If this object exists, as I believe it does, Mr Fenby, and is in the possession of your wife, then it is likely to be worth a considerable sum of money.'

A pause again. A deliberate oiling of the trap. Bran held his breath. His father must hold out.

The stranger's voice again. 'But as I have told you, I ask for no more than I should be allowed to make an examination. To prove its existence is my main concern, as an historian. If I should make an offer, then that is an entirely different matter and the decision is completely up to your wife and yourself. I shall not attempt to persuade.'

Keep quiet. Say nothing. Bran willed his father not to let the stranger into his mother's secrets. The pause lengthened. He longed for her to speak; she would know what to say. But it was his father.

'Well, Alice. It's up to you.'

That was enough. The stranger knew. But the trap had sprung in silence. There was no more than a rustle as some person in the room rose and moved towards the door.

Swiftly, without noise himself, Bran backed away along the passage and by the time the door opened he was through the kitchen and leaving the house.

5

Stella sat in the long grass on the bank below the towpath. Slightly above her, Sandy lay spreadeagled under the sun.

'Your father,' said Sandy.

'What about him?' The girl hugged her knees and watched where a fly dipped into the still water of the canal and rippled the huge horizontal picture of trees and sky.

'I don't think he likes me.'

The dark girl said nothing.

'Stella? Did you hear what I said?' Sandy raised herself on one elbow in time to see the girl nod. 'Well don't you care?'

'I might if I thought it was true.'

'It is.' Sandy nipped off a long stem of grass, concentrating on the way her nails bit into the fleshy green. 'He doesn't like me at all.'

'I suppose you have a reason for saying that.'

'It might surprise you to know that I have.' Sandy let herself fall back. 'It's because he treats me so respectfully.'

Stella gave a small snort of laughter but did not turn towards her. 'Well what do you expect?' she said. 'You are the boss's daughter.'

'Sod it.'

'As you say,' said Stella.

'When I called for you just now' – Sandy had put

the stem of grass between her teeth and was squinting up at its feathery head against the sky – 'and you weren't there, he called me Miss Alexandra. He even walked all the way down the path to open the gate for me, and all the time he called me Miss Alexandra. Will you tell him he needn't do that?'

'Very well, Miss Alexandra.'

'Oh, Christ.' Sandy rolled over and clasped her hands over her hair. 'I've said the wrong bloody thing again.'

'Several times. You needn't swear just because you're down here among us.'

Sandy, her face to the grass, did not move for a long moment. Then she unclasped her hands and raised herself on both elbows. 'I think you hate me as well.'

'Not you.'

'Well you don't like the things I say.'

Stella turned towards her, drawing in her breath, about to speak. But she paused, changed her mind, and turned away.

'Don't say anything, then,' said Sandy.

Stella hugged her legs closer and rested her chin on her knees. The truth was that the sight of Sandy had dazzled her. Under the shining red-gold hair the teeth and lips glinted, the small red tongue flickered as she smiled, and the sheen of her thin green dress threw back the light like water. She was a glittering serpent, and Stella knew herself to be no more than her dowdy victim.

'I'm bored.' The green dress slid along the grass as she stretched herself.

'You've no need to be.'

'I know. I've got everything. People are always telling me.'

'Well haven't you?'

'I haven't got what you've got. I haven't got a boyfriend in the village. Mine's miles away and I shan't see him all this holiday.'

'There's others.'

'Stella Grey I'm surprised at you.' But she was sitting up, grinning. 'Who, for instance?'

'Take your pick. You know you could have any one you wanted.'

'Except your Griff.'

'Even him. He's more your type than mine.'

'Stella!'

'It's the truth.'

'You're a fool, Stella Grey. There's no need ever to say things like that.'

'Even if they're true?'

'Especially if they're true.'

Stella was silent, not even responding to cynicism, and Sandy, leaning on one elbow, examined her profile. There was nothing wrong with Stella's looks except that already she seemed more of a woman than a girl. She was solemn. Her mouth was well shaped but it had a downward twist to it and, as now, she had the habit of looking away from whoever was with her as if some more important matter was on her mind. You never knew where you were with her. Poor Griff. Yet her eyes were so marvellous; that deep blue and those dark lashes. They could do things to Griff if they ever stayed on him long enough. I wonder if . . .

'You are a whirlpool, Sandy.' Stella spoke without turning her head. 'You swirl around and everything swirls with you. And there you are, right in the middle, pulling everything towards you. I've not seen anybody escape yet.'

Sandy sat up on her heels. 'Is that a compliment?'

'Please yourself.'

'There you go again! You never say exactly what you mean.'

'Not like you.'

'Not like me.'

The dark girl took it no further and Sandy, wanting to continue a burst that promised intimacy, was left looking at the long, almost black hair that lay carelessly on the shoulders of the blue dress. She took a comb from her pocket and began gently to tease out the tangles at Stella's back.

'I wish I had hair your colour. Then people would be able to see my eyebrows. I've got a face like a pink pig.'

Stella laughed and Sandy was encouraged. 'But if I did have hair like this I would take more care of it.' And the blue of her dress could be a tone darker to make her eyes deeper; and she ought to do something about those scuff marks on her shoes. If she had a mother it would be different. She felt a twinge of pity. 'I could get your hair really nice.'

'Don't bother. You have to spend enough time on your own.'

'Nasty.'

'It succeeds. All the boys flock round.'

'I've never noticed it.'

'You dazzle them and you know it.'

'But not Griff; no matter what you say.' The comb was taking long silken sweeps. 'What's he like? You know what I mean. What's he really like?'

Stella knew what was required. Sandy had often enough demonstrated from her own experiences what she wanted to hear: the long, triumphant descriptions of intimacies both inflicted and welcomed; the repetition of secrets whispered in such moments; the hidden peculiarities and passions.

Sandy, anticipating, giggled impatiently and the comb tugged, forcing Stella to lift her chin so that she found herself looking down her cheeks towards the water. It was just possible she might indulge Sandy. The truth could be teased out enough to excite her. But it was pleasant to hold her in suspense, be served by her. It was as though she herself was a queen on the vast green throne of the bank and Sandy was her attendant. The water was polished stone beyond her feet, and the huge trees that rose from the other bank were the lofty roof and distant corridors of her palace.

'You had a visitor,' she said. She was regal, deliberately perverse.

'Did we?' Sandy had her mind elsewhere.

'An elderly man in grey.'

'You don't miss much, do you?'

'I saw him cross the lock gates.' Every visitor to the house on the hill had to do that. Stella and her father lived in the lock-keeper's cottage. 'I was in our garden and he raised his hat to me.'

Sandy laughed. She had been diverted from her earlier preoccupation but this was just as amusing. 'Wasn't he sweet? Didn't he have nice little eyes? Like a lovely little monkey. All wizened and fierce. My mother hated him.'

'Why?'

It was a legitimate question but Sandy hesitated. 'Oh I don't know. Keep your head down. They didn't take to each other, I suppose.'

But Stella had noted the reluctance in her reply and knew that something was being hidden. Once again she was being made to keep her place, a villager, not permitted to know in detail what happened in the house on the hill. But her hair was being gathered and smoothed behind her and she permitted herself to become a prize animal having her sleek back groomed ready to be shown and paraded. There was a disturbing pleasure in it that soothed her resentment and allowed her to be calm. She spoke to the ground.

'He stayed at the Black Swan last night.' She could be expected to know that because Griff was the landlord's son. 'Griff said he wanted to buy something from them.'

'I'm not surprised. That's what he's here for. He's an antique dealer.' Sandy slid the comb through the hair for the last time. 'There you are; that's done.'

She was dismissing the subject of the visitor, but Stella would not permit it. 'He came to buy something of yours, did he?'

'Some of my father's pots.'

'They're not antiques.'

'Well there's plenty of old junk around as well.'

'In your place. There's nothing he'd want to buy in mine.'

'You don't know.'

'We don't have anything like that picture in the museum, for instance.'

It was an attempt to direct the conversation and it succeeded.

'Why do you say that?' asked Sandy.

Stella shrugged and did not answer.

'Well that picture is one thing he can't have because my father's practically given it to the village now, the idiot.'

'So that was what he wanted.'

Sandy had revealed more than she intended and knew it. 'That, and something else.' She stood up. 'But he can't have it, not even as a gift.' She looked down and saw Stella's eyes on her, calmly awaiting an explanation. She spun round. 'Because it's not my father's to throw away.' As she said the words she lifted her hand over her head and sent her comb spinning out across the water. 'Like that.'

Stella followed the comb's flight and saw the splash. Sandy laughed. The diversion was enough to change the subject.

'Lunch time,' she said, and began to walk away. 'See you later.'

Stella watched the medallion of spreading rings where the comb had disappeared. The tiny waves, moving outwards, momentarily broke the reflection of the sky and left her gazing through a hole in its skin. She waited until it had closed and then she too moved away.

The square was deserted in the heat of the day, but it was cool in the little museum. She stood for a long time in front of the picture that had so interested the man she had followed.

6

Bran watched the red second hand sweep around the face of the kitchen clock. Its endless circles, retreating as the world moved, corkscrewed away through space, a thin spiral into which he let himself fall, drifting further and further into infinity as the thread tightened around him. But there was no escape from the present. The voice in the kitchen insisted on an audience.

'Ah, tea,' said his father, 'that is a consummation devoutly to be wished.'

Not even his own words. Why can't he speak for himself? Bran lowered his eyes from the clock on the wall.

His father made up for lack of height with a stately head. He had a fine, large nose, large ears, a generous, easy mouth and a structure of deep, emphatic wrinkles, all of which was now thrust forward in an elaborate comic stoop as he advanced on the table, rubbing his hands like a miser.

'A sumptuous repast,' he said. 'Tarts and jams and fruit cake, honey from the bee, and delicious morsels from foreign parts.'

'Sardines,' said his wife.

'Adequate,' he said, 'and more. More than adequate.'

'That's enough, George.'

He pecked her on the cheek and straightened as

her plump form patiently pushed him aside and made for the kettle steaming in the corner.

'And how fares my son this golden evening?'

'All right,' said Bran.

'Good. Good. I am delighted to hear it.' He was turning away as he spoke and taking off his jacket of speckled fawn which he placed with great precision on a coat hanger and hung on the kitchen door. Next, as always, he ran the fingernails of both hands along the sides of his head to make sure that the thin grey hair was not overlapping the earpieces of his glasses. Then, as he stepped towards the kitchen sink, pulling up his shirt sleeves so that the armbands he wore held the cuffs clear of his wrists, he looked once more towards his son.

'So the long vac has commenced, if that's the phrase preferred,' he said. 'How goes it?'

Bran began a wince that was genuine but, so as not to offend, made it into a grimace intended to amuse. 'Summer holiday is the phrase preferred,' he said.

'Whatever the nomenclature,' the creases deepened to intensify the twinkle in his father's eyes, 'there are seven endless weeks of sunshine ahead.'

'Work. I've got a lot of reading to do.'

His mother placed the teapot in the centre of the table. 'I haven't seen him all day,' she said. 'He's been up in his room. I only hope he's made his bed.'

Bran did not answer and she did not seek a reply but busied herself, in her slow way, with placing other things on the table. He watched his father's ritual. There was first of all the soaping of the hands, then the hooking of them together, nails hidden in palms, and the working up of a thin lather. It was precise, neat, and, Bran knew from trying it, not very efficient.

'Hurry up, George.'

'I won't be a moment, my dear.'

'I know your moments.'

The large, splendid head had all day dignified a clerk's desk in the upstairs office of a building materials supplier in a narrow street behind the market place. Now it was inclined over the kitchen taps overseeing the rinsing. The hands were dried so that the thin-framed spectacles could be removed from the large nose, and then the hands were once more wetted and soaped to wash the face. It was always the same apparently public procedure but it was too intimate for Bran ever to have asked why the hands had to be washed twice, so he and his mother waited in silence while the face in its turn was subjected to soap and water and the towel was picked up.

'Ablutions completed,' said his father. 'The dust of the day's labours removed.'

'I've been waiting long enough,' said his wife. She was more than usually irritated by his precision. 'As you're so fussy, George, I wonder you don't go upstairs to wash instead of drying your face on the kitchen towel.'

'Convenience, my love. The distances between the necessary facilities in this house are large.'

'Well it's always been so. I should have thought you'd have come to some better arrangement by now.'

'I have grown accustomed to it. It no longer bothers me.'

'Well it does me. Your tea's poured.'

Bran knew what was coming next – the house. His mother's dissatisfaction and his father's blandness in the face of it always had the same result. Nothing would change. They were caught, all of them, in this narrow house, squeezed by its neighbours in a crawling ant-run of a street. Bran hated it and so did she.

44

'It's dark in here,' said his mother. She switched on the light before she sat down at the table. 'It's that one little window. And that yard.'

The kitchen faced the wall of the next house and between them there was a tiny paved area divided by a tall wooden fence. The sun reached there only at dawn and it was never warm.

'I wouldn't mind,' she said, 'if we had something like a garden.'

Normally she was placid, but from time to time a great gloom would descend on her and her brooding would drag them all with her. But this evening she was challenged.

'It could change, Alice.' Her husband looked across the table at her. 'It could all be different, you know.'

This was something new. Bran had heard his father many times preaching the virtue of making do with what they could afford; now he was talking as though their circumstances had changed.

'It's entirely in your hands, my dear.'

She poured her husband's tea and then Bran's, but did not fill her own cup. Even this was a comment; a measure of resentment.

'You have only to say the word.' Boyishness erased the dignity of the face. There was excitement in his smile. 'The key is in your hands.'

She remained rounded and smooth and expressionless. She held by one corner a tiny piece of bread and butter poised over her plate. She raised it to her mouth and Bran was angered with her for eating when she should have answered. She chewed delicately, both hands lifeless in her lap.

'What's going on?' said Bran.

His father, still smiling, looked at his mother.

'You'd best ask your father,' she said. 'He seems to

have made up his mind. It's nothing to do with me.'

'Now, Alice, you know I am not going to interfere. The decision is yours, and yours alone.' Still she did not respond, and after a moment he said, 'Shall I tell him?'

'If you like.'

He patted her hand, winked at his son and left the kitchen. There was silence while he was out of the room, and even when he returned she said nothing. He was carrying something which he held in one hand while he cleared a space among the tea things and put it down.

Then he stood back.

'That,' he said, 'is worth a lot of money.'

Bran doubted it. The little box that now stood in the centre of the table had always had a place on the mantlepiece in his parents' bedroom flanked by the green glass candlesticks that never held a candle. His mother had used it for hairpins and tarnished necklaces.

'Enough money to take your mother out of this kitchen for good.'

Bran nodded, humouring him. This was one of his father's enthusiasms. He had read something somewhere and jumped to a conclusion. The box, no higher than a teacup, was made of a heavy dark wood, deeply carved, the scrolls of its lid overhanging the sides and matching its ornate base. It was a copy of something medieval, and overdone.

'We had a visitor last night.' His father was smiling. 'A traveller from an antique land.'

'I know,' said Bran. 'I heard him.'

'Did you indeed? Well this is what brought him to us.'

The little box squatted like a black toad near his

mother's hand, seeming to press into the tablecloth with twice its true weight. She had almost ignored it until now, but suddenly she was accusing his father. 'You should never have let him know about it. It's none of his business.'

'Nor mine, Alice.' He was taken aback for a moment, but then his smile returned. 'It belongs to you. But he knew it existed. Or at least he guessed. Your sister might have told him.'

'She had no right! We were always told never to tell anyone. We promised when we were little girls.'

Her eyes were full of tears, and her husband went to her, put his arm around her shoulder, and looked at Bran over her head. 'Your son is mystified, my dear.'

She had taken a handkerchief and was wiping the corners of her eyes. 'I'm stupid,' she said. 'It's super-stitious. But it's all I've got left of the old days. And Martha and I swore that we'd never ever sell. They said it was bad luck.' She tried to smile at herself.

'Your mother is telling you, Bran, that this is a family heirloom.'

'My grandmother said it belonged to her grand-mother. It's always belonged to the women.'

'Hence the superstition.' Her husband patted her shoulder. 'But it has long since been played out. Nothing to worry about now.'

'That's easy for you to say. You haven't had to live with it all these years.'

'Long enough, Alice, long enough.' He picked up the box to examine it, turning it in his hands. He began to smile. 'Alice,' he said, 'I believe this little object speaks for itself.'

She did not comprehend.

'Don't you remember what it says?' He held it closer to her and revolved it slowly so that she could see each of its sides in turn. The deeply carved foliage was entwined around columns and arches so that the long sides had four bays and the ends each had two, and in each bay a tall capital letter stood amid the black leaves. He read out the words they made: IN TIME OF NEED. 'There, Alice' – he put it down in front of her – 'it is practically offering itself. Your time of need has come.'

She fingered it uncertainly. 'But I promised.'

'You were only a little girl. Times have changed.'

'I know, but . . .'

Bran could bear to see the conflict in her no longer. 'Don't sell it,' he said.

The eyes she turned on him had expanded darkly and the lips in her round, soft face trembled. She looked very young. She was shaking her head as she spoke. 'But you don't know how much he said it was worth, Bran. It was a lot of money.'

'I don't care!' Love for her swept over him and he was reckless. 'Don't even tell me.'

'But it's for you and your father. You don't like being here and it would make so much difference.'

'And make you unhappy,' he said. 'It can't be worth that.'

He caught his father's eye and saw the pleasure there.

'Alice, that's the sort of son you have! Who needs money?'

She had bowed her head and was trying not to weep. 'I'm being silly,' she said. 'I know I am.'

'It's not silly to do the right thing.'

'But so much. I can't throw away so much.'

'But we can, can't we, Bran?' He enjoyed the extravagance, and his voice became increasingly loud. 'We'll turn him down flat when he comes back. We'll tell him: the last thing we need in all the world is money, *anybody's* money, *your* money!'

Bran laughed with him. 'The big gesture, Dad.'

'The big gesture, Bran. And listen – what makes it all so marvellous is that a man like that, that man in particular, will not understand it at all. We will be the bafflement of him.'

'I know,' said Bran. 'I heard him.'

'You weren't there, my boy.'

'I was. Outside the door.' Bran felt shame. 'I'm sorry.'

But his father laughed; forgiveness was instant. 'Did you hear that, Alice? He was ahead of us all the time.'

She had not been listening. Now she stood up between them. 'I've made up my mind,' she said.

'It's all three of us together,' he said. 'We'll tell Mr Harman a thing or two.'

'I'm going to sell.'

She shocked him. 'No, Alice. Not now.'

'Particularly now.' She spoke almost shyly, looking at neither of them. 'Both of you have already given up all that money. Because of me. You never thought twice. Now I'm going to do something for you.'

They both spoke together but she silenced them, putting out her hands and grasping each of them by the arm. 'It's no good trying to stop me. I've made up my mind.' She was smiling at both of them, and her husband put his arms around her.

7

It was dusk on the hill and the sky was dusted with summer stars. The telephone, submerged in the warm darkness of the hall, rang with an underwater sound that barely disturbed Sandy in her room. In the quietness between the rings she heard her mother's dress rustle past her door as she went to answer it, and then her voice.

'Yes?'

Her father opened the door of his study.

'Speaking,' said her mother softly.

Silence. Then a slithering, urgent sound as though her mother had sat down quickly, and her father's footstep in the hall.

It was late. Bran sat in the front room waiting to hear their footsteps in the street outside. They had gone out early in the evening, keen to be away, ready to enjoy themselves now the decision had been made. He himself had done the washing up while his father went to fetch the car from the lock-up garage and bring it to the end of the street, and his mother had changed into the newest of her dresses.

'Come with us, Bran,' she had said. 'It doesn't seem right to celebrate without you.'

'Just you and Dad. Enjoy yourselves. You're entitled.'

Doubt had again clouded her eyes. 'We have done the right thing, haven't we?'

For once he had consciously imitated his father, brushing aside her apprehensions. 'To look at you now nobody would believe you were old enough to have a son my age.'

'With all this grey in my hair?' She had tilted her head yet again in front of the hallway mirror.

'Fashionable. You've put it in deliberately.'

She had turned. 'Come here and I'll give you a big wet kiss.'

She had put her hands on his shoulders and pulled his face down towards her. Her dress had a wardrobe smell, but there was an odour he had forgotten. On Sunday mornings, when he was small, he would creep into her bed and lie between her and his father. That warm cavern of absolute ease and safety had engulfed him again.

'Just this one night.' She had kissed him. 'See you later.'

He had gone to the front window to watch her as, blushing slightly and from time to time quickening her step in her excitement so that for a few paces she was almost trotting, she had fluttered in her finery along the street.

He had spent the evening reading, but now it was getting dark. They could not be much longer, and he went to the kitchen to put the kettle on. The object that was the cause of the celebration still rested on the table where they had left it. It was typical of his father to be careless with objects of value, and his mother had seemed to want nothing more to do with the casket.

'Casket,' he said aloud, remembering that she had disliked the word when he used it earlier. 'But that's what it is; an empty casket.'

A kind of superstition, or perhaps the effect of his father's disdain, had made him also ignore the box until this moment. Now he picked it up. It was heavier than its size indicated, and he began to examine it for the first time in many years. It was really quite beautiful. The overhanging lid was carved to form foliage that drooped over the arches along its sides as though from the roof of an arbour, and the letters between the pillars gave the appearance of being inside, under shelter.

He lifted the lid. The casket was empty but not as deep as it seemed from outside, and this was a clue to its weight for the bottom was not, like the rest, made of wood but was a rectangle of glazed pottery. This must have been a whim of the old potter to whom it had belonged; perhaps it was this that gave it its value. He turned it over and the thick pottery tile moved slightly in its grooves but still, after two centuries, it fitted snugly enough to be in no danger of falling out. The same pale greenish sheen glimmered at him from between the four squat legs as it had from the shadows of the interior.

He looked inside again. The pottery base was an oddity he had never thought about. His mother had never told him what the casket might have contained.

'It's because she never liked it, I suppose,' he said to the empty room. And it was, perhaps, faintly sinister, but the green glaze made it less so. And then there was its value. This small object could buy a house. 'The kind of house,' he said aloud, 'which might have a few things like this scattered around in it.'

The thought made him laugh. Then he shrugged, closed the lid and turned his back on it as he went upstairs with his tea.

*

Sandy heard her father's voice above the murmur of her mother at the telephone.

'What is it, Martha?'

She strained her ears but could hear no reply. She slid off the edge of the bed and went to the stairhead. Nobody had switched on a light and it was dark in the hall.

'Martha?'

Then her mother's voice clung to the air like the last grey gleam in the fanlight over the door; the same word over and over. 'No. No. No.'

'What is it, Martha?'

'Alice and George.' The words came faintly, on the edge of a gasp. 'They're dead.'

8

The man standing in the darkness on the doorstep was recognizable as a policeman only by the glint of the silver numbers on his shoulder. He wore no cap, knowing already he would have to enter.

'Bernard Fenby?'

'Yes.' Bran acknowledged his formal name.

'May I come in, Mr Fenby?'

The house was empty at Bran's back and he retreated into it, hearing the boards of the hallway creak and echo up the stairs as the policeman entered.

'Thank you, Mr Fenby.' Then, 'Have you any relatives living nearby, son?'

Son. The word floated between them for him to grasp if needed.

'No.'

'Shall we go in here?' The policeman indicated the door to the front room, opened it and courteously stood back.

'What is it?' Bran heard his own words as thin as wires in the air. He had no breath.

The policeman searched and found the light switch. 'I have some bad news for you, son.' His face jumped out of the darkness; watchful eyes, a determined mouth. 'There's been an accident.'

The nightmare had come.

The policeman, expecting him to sway, put out a

hand, but Bran had already pressed his back against the doorpost.

Conventional words emerged. 'I'm all right,' he said.

The dark uniform went ahead of him into the room.

'It's your parents, son.' Once more the friendly arm, but Bran was already sitting. The material of the chair cover was cold, even through his clothes. 'That's right, Bernard; you sit down.'

Cold through and through and through; cold to the centre; I am marble. My thoughts are a skin on the surface of the marble; I am leaving, I am leaving, I am leaving.

His eyes tilted upwards and he saw that the policeman had found the exact centre of the room. Nightmare exactitude. The light was directly over his head. The only shadow he cast was at his feet. There was no need for anybody to move again.

Bran opened his mouth. His lips peeled softly apart and the catch of the silence was released.

'I'm afraid they're dead, son.'

Thus the policeman. Then himself.

'Both of them?'

He had to get his accounting right; he had to make sure of the colossal total.

'I'm sorry, son. Their car and a lorry. They couldn't have known anything about it.'

'Oh.'

The brightness of the room startled him. Chairs, curtains, clocks were sharp-edged. They clamoured. They came for him. They fought for his brain like ugly, greedy children, all at once, dazzling, shouting, crowding towards him until he fell back in front of them. He looked up, mouth open, as a black, vile surge of darkness rescued him from the tumult.

9

Days followed. He did not know where he was. Shutters had clapped to and closed off vistas, boarded up the ends of streets, shut out the sky, boxed him in a wooden universe. He walked and walked in a grey light on a long planked floor yet never reached the walls.

He wore what was put out for him, went in a car that shone as black as a beetle to where ugly glittering flowers were piled in a hideous mound that stank of sweet decay, and heard people sob and talk in room after room that were all part of the same room.

All in the sunshine.

And then it was another place. Cooler. On a hillside. It rained and the woods around the house wept as he lay, fully clothed, on a strange bed.

10

There was a tap on the door and a girl's voice.

'Are you there?'

He stirred for answer.

'Do you want to go out? It's stopped raining.'

He sat on the edge of the bed. 'Yes,' he said, meaning only that he had noticed that the sun dappled the window-ledge.

'I'll wait for you downstairs. Don't be long.'

His cousin went away and he crossed the room to the wash-basin in the corner. He soaped his hands and rinsed them. Then he filled the bowl, cupped water in his hands and buried his face. The water was cool and soothed the aching muscles of his cheeks and around his eyes. He raised his head and faced the mirror but did not see himself; his eyes had learned to avoid the loneliness of his reflection. But he saw the room behind him, made miniature, as in a picture. There was a greenish light, because of the trees outside, and a softly receding dimness in which the furniture was at rest.

He turned, with the towel at his chin, and saw the room for the first time. It was large and low-ceilinged. Beyond the foot of the big bed there was still enough space for a circular table with chairs standing in the centre of a fringed carpet. Along the foot of the bed there was a couch for daytime resting and reading, and a massive wardrobe stood guard in the dimmest corner. There was distance between every object yet everything held together, contained within the warmth of the house.

His mother had been on her best behaviour here, long ago. He remembered it; and his father's pleasure, simply happy with the comfort of the place.

He stepped out of the corner, and the sun on the carpet warmed his feet and legs and rose to enclose him. He was thinking of them without any effort and they were almost there. He let them appear in the air around him and was unfocused and content.

Water trickled on his neck and he moved the towel. Tiny motes shone in the sunlight around him; nothing else. He held the towel up to his face and wept.

She stood near the foot of the stairs where the sun, striking through the coloured glass panels above and at the sides of the door, enriched the pattern of the carpet. She was grinning.

'You're wet,' she said.

'I can't help it. I was born that way.' His words caught them both by surprise and she laughed.

'I didn't mean that,' she said. 'It's your shirt.'

He looked down and saw that he had splashed his collar and the front of his shirt as he washed. He began to climb the stairs, intending to change, but she called after him, 'It doesn't matter about that. Come with me.'

Sandy had her arm outstretched and was flickering her fingers impatiently to draw him towards her. He came down and she grasped his hand and began pulling him behind her through the hall to the back of the house. There was a glass-panelled door, then a dim passage leading to another, and beyond it a wide glass conservatory.

'Stifling,' she said, and they crossed it quickly to emerge on to a paved area where small flowering plants grew through the cracks. She breathed deeply and slammed the door behind them. 'Fresh air!'

Raindrops shaken from the gutter splashed on to their arms and drew their eyes to their clasped hands.

She released him. 'I'm going to take my shoes off.' She stepped out of her sandals and stooped to pick them up. 'You can do the same if you like.'

He shook his head.

'Please yourself.'

The garden rose up the hill in a series of terraces, gigantic steps that gradually diminished and became less laden with flowers until eventually they were swallowed up by the forest.

He stood, looking up, aware that he was taking an interest in something outside himself. He would let her know. 'It's nice,' he said. 'I like it.'

'You're not obliged to.' She began to climb the stone steps that led to the next level. 'Race you!' – and she was halfway across the lawn before he got to the top.

He followed, but she was much faster, grasping her sandals as though each was a relay racer's baton and leaping the steps as she came to them.

He slipped on the wet lawn and fell full length. She paused on the terrace above to look down and laugh at him. He got halfway to his feet, crouching like a sprinter.

'Right,' he said. 'Now you're for it.'

'If you can catch me, Blondie.' She turned and vanished.

He ran up the steps, crossed the next lawn, plunged into the narrow space between two bushes where the next steps lay and leapt them, expecting to have gained on her, but she was higher still. He gulped air and ran, but he was clumsy and she knew the ground, and when he reached the fifth and final tier where the garden, having no formal edge, petered out beneath the trees, she was nowhere to be seen.

Panting, he turned to look down. The roof of the house lay among a froth of flowers like the bottom of a boat turned over by the green wave of the hillside. The village was out of sight below and the canal kept to the coolness of the trees and was hidden. The house was halfway up an escarpment beyond which the plain spread out, patched with yellow and green and diminishing into the tiny patterns of a snake's skin on which, far out, an occasional car glinted like a bead of moisture.

But nothing here was his. The excitement of the chase drained suddenly from him. He was not entitled to this. He turned away and was about to wander aimlessly until she should find him, when he saw the dark marks of her track leading across the glittering lawn to the trees on his right.

A path followed a contour among the knotted, slippery roots, but the slope fell steeply away and walking was difficult. Soon he was hot and having to concentrate on every step so that when the sun, which until then had only penetrated the topmost layers high overhead, suddenly fell full on him he raised his head and was surprised to find he was at the edge of the trees.

He stopped to draw breath and saw her. She seemed for a moment to have walked straight out from the hillside and to be floating in mid-air. The sky at her back was also beneath her feet. Vertigo made him cringe, wanting to draw back, and even when he saw that the blue emptiness under her feet was the sky's reflection in a rock pool she was still held out into space on a giddy ledge.

She was grinning. 'Come and look,' she said. She took a step towards him and her bare feet disappeared into the pool. 'Come on, Bran.' The bright surface rippled like mercury around her ankles, spreading out as though she waded through it in the sky.

She called out to him again. 'Take your shoes off and come with me.'

He remained where he was.

'You weren't like this when you were a kid,' she said.

'Like what?'

She pressed her lips together as though she was trying not to giggle. 'Don't you remember, Randy Brandy?'

'Remember what?'

She looked at him from under her eye-lashes but said nothing. Shame flooded him, and then excitement. He remembered well enough, but had buried the memory. They had been very young and curious about each other, and what had happened belonged to that time, not now. Too much had changed. They themselves were different, but here she was pretending otherwise. He could only stare at her, but after a few seconds she took her eyes from him and raised her head so that the light from the water flickered on her neck and beneath her chin.

'Well if you don't remember you don't remember and there's no point in talking about it.' She turned away to splash across the pool, scattering drops of silver as she went.

He found his voice. 'Tell me!' he shouted after her, but she ignored him until she stepped out of the pool on the other side.

'Come over here, Brandywine, and I'll show you Potter Waterfall's Steps.'

'Damn Potter Waterfall's Steps!'

She was maddening, blandly pretending she did not notice his frustration. 'You'll have to take your shoes and socks off,' she said.

He stepped straight into the water and she shouted with laughter. Now, at last, she was paying attention. He splashed towards her, sending the spray high, careless of where it fell, and suddenly she fled from him, swinging around, seeming to lose her balance, and plunging into space. She vanished beneath the edge, out of sight, falling away.

The sickening feeling of a new tragedy swept over him and he ran the last few steps. Suddenly he was on the rock at the pool's edge and was at a giddy height. But she had fooled him. A few feet below there was a ledge of moss, and beyond it more ledges sinking away steeply until they reached the final immense drop. He was at the top of Potter Waterfall's Steps and she was bounding from ledge to ledge below him. Sometimes her whole figure showed up against the crawling plain as though the plunge had begun and his flesh shrank to the bone. But always she was safe, and then she paused, looked back to make sure he was there, and an instant later was lost to sight beneath an overhang.

He waited but she did not reappear, and gradually he began to take in the true nature of the Steps. They were broad platforms, made green by moss, in which other pools lay like blue mirrors or velvet pits. They were a rocky outcrop made into a hanging garden.

He began to zig-zag down between humps of moss, occasionally scattering a pool as he went from ledge to ledge and knowing that, seen from above, his own figure would now be standing out against the plain, but never in any danger on the wide levels.

He did not see her until she was in front of him, no more than a few yards away. She was reclining, resting on the steps of a little wooden summerhouse set back against the rock wall, and she was looking at him, ready to laugh, her eyes screwed up against the sun. He did his best to ignore her, and crossed the moss to sit down alongside her. He began to take off his shoes.

'You're crazy,' she said.

'One of us is.' He peeled off his socks, let them fall and sat holding his wet trousers away from his legs. He looked across the platform. It reached out seven or eight yards from them and was overlapped in several places to give it different levels. Rock plants growing between the pools were humped like the heads and shoulders of climbers coming up from below so that he found his eyes darting from place to place as he seemed to catch a movement on the edge of his vision.

She understood what was happening. 'Don't worry,' she said, 'nobody comes here.'

'Did Potter Waterfall?'

'Of course he did. Didn't my father tell you this is where the old boy used to come to sit and think? He bores most people with it.'

He turned towards her. 'I don't remember this place at all.'

'Liar.' Her eyes glinted, refusing to let him look away. 'You remember very well.'

'The hut,' he said. 'I think I remember the hut.'

'I should think you do.'

'But not all this.' He swept his arm towards the Steps and the space beyond. 'This is all new.'

She giggled. 'That was Stella,' she said. 'She

blindfolded you because all this was supposed to be secret. Especially from you; especially from a boy.'

'But there wasn't anybody else.' He was certain. 'There couldn't have been.'

'Not inside the hut,' said Sandy. 'She lost her nerve. Just you and me.'

The faintly musty smell of the warm, dim hut came back to him, and the clumsiness with which, daring each other, they had each taken off their clothes, standing far apart. How white and slender she was, how skinny himself. And their hungry eyes as they stood before each other. He had forgotten nothing, except the girl outside.

'She knocked on the door just in time,' said Sandy.

'I never went near you. I didn't even kiss you. I wanted to, but I was afraid.'

'Of me?'

'Yes.'

'You needn't have been.' She had let her head roll sideways so that her cheek pressed against her shoulder and her lips were forced slightly apart like a pouting child's.

He leant towards her and she did not move. 'It's all a blank after that,' he said. 'I must have been led away blindfold again.'

The wet trousers clung to his legs as he lowered his face. His shadow fell on her eyelids but she did not stir until his lips touched the corner of her mouth. Then she opened her eyes wide and rolled her head so that her mouth was full on his, soft and wet. Her head made little shaking movements as though she wanted him fiercely and quickly. And then just as suddenly she let her head fall back.

'Cheat,' she said.

'You wanted me to do it.'

64

Suddenly she pushed him away and stood up looking down at him. Her eyes had a greenish glitter. 'Where did you get those clothes?'

He shrugged, caught off guard.

'Grey socks, grey trousers, grey pullover.' Her chant turned to laughter. 'You're not the pretty little boy you used to be. You look like some kid just starting school.'

He had worn what anybody put out for him and had not noticed or cared. Now he saw that he was dressed for emptiness; a subdued, extended mourning.

'If you're going to be my lover,' she said, 'you'll have to dress better than that.'

Suddenly she was running between the clumps of moss, climbing back up the slopes. It was an invitation to him to give chase again, but the hollowness had returned, and with it the lethargy. She was out of sight when he began to follow.

I I

Stella came out of the shop and stood under the blind. It was mid-morning and the sun had climbed high enough to make the shadows retreat from the open spaces and curl as black as a cat under the trees in the centre of the square. Beyond it the door of the Black Swan stood open and rubber mats from the bar lay on the paving outside where they had been scrubbed and left to dry. Griff's work; helping his father.

Two weeks into the holiday and the routine was set. Shopping, the mid-morning meeting with Griff, then housework, and lunch to prepare for her father. She breathed out slowly. Boredom seemed to increase with the intensity of the sun and she half-closed her eyes against it. Sandy would be welcome; even flirting with Griff. But it wouldn't happen; hadn't happened since the accident. Sandy had tried, but failed, to hide the joy that the tragedy gave her; the lopping off of an aunt and uncle, and the sudden acquisition to her household of a boy. He had become a blond, tragic figure that nobody was allowed to see. She was as secretive over him as with all her other possessions.

There was a movement far back in the darkness of the Black Swan's interior and Stella swung her shopping bag, preparing to step forward. But it was not Griff who emerged. The short, grey figure who occupied the pavement and stood unblinking in the sunshine, was Harman. She knew the name because Sandy had revealed it, grudgingly. He was another of her secrets, her hoarded privileges.

Stella drew back under the shade of the blind. Harman stood motionless, his hat squarely on his head, his hands behind his back, and surveyed the square as though it was laid out for his inspection. In a moment he would move, and she knew in which direction he would go. The only business he could have was with the house on the hill, and then Sandy would have more to hint at and gloat over. Unless . . .

Before the thought had properly formed in her head Stella was moving, walking swiftly along the side of the square until the grove hid her from Harman, and then she broke into a trot.

The keys to the museum were kept in the parish clerk's office and she ran up the steps of the hall without looking back. There was an agony of waiting inside until the keys were found and she feared he would be mounting the steps as she went down, but when she came out and stood between the pillars he was nowhere in sight. She had miscalculated; he was not so much a creature of habit as she had assumed and the museum held no further interest for him.

But now, with the keys in her hand, her own course had been decided. Angry with herself, she entered the alley and let herself into the museum.

The narrow anteroom, out of the sun, was cold, and as the inner swing doors closed themselves behind her the movement of the air on her bare arms made her shiver. She was relieved, now, that she had been mistaken about Harman. The thought that he could have come in at her back, trapping her in this chill mausoleum, made her struggle not to shudder again, and to remove him from her mind she clattered swiftly

67

across the black and white tiles to bend over the display cabinet beneath the picture.

The few objects spaced out under the glass bored her; she had seen them all before; but automatically she raised her eyes to compare them with the picture. It was then, through the tall side window, that she glimpsed a movement at the end of the alley. Something had made the transition from light to shade.

She ceased to breathe. She knew that her fear was quite unreasoned but it had her in its grip. She did not even dare to turn her head. All of her attention was concentrated in the corner of her eye. The shape glided smoothly nearer and vanished behind her. Then she heard the furtive scuff of feet on the steps outside and knew that now he was within the vestibule, regarding her through the glass doors.

She held herself still. All she could do was pretend that she was absorbed in what was before her, oblivious of what was happening.

The hinges sighed faintly as the door opened and space yawned at her back. Still she remained rigid.

And then the leather sole of a foot clicked on a tile and she could pretend no longer. She spun round.

'I startled you,' he said.

'No.' The word jerked from her almost like an accusation.

From under the brim of the hat the eyes turned towards her were the sightless pits of a marble bust. 'Forgive me.' As if in courtesy he removed his hat, but the effect was to let light play upon his eyes. They were yellow, and had an unseeing, reptilian glare.

'I was just about to go,' she said. 'I've seen all I wanted.' She took a step but he made no effort to move aside and she stopped, almost in the middle of the floor, with her shopping bag clutched in front of her.

He said nothing.

'I come here a lot.' She heard words coming from herself, making excuses when none should have been needed. 'The picture . . . It belongs to a friend of mine; used to belong, anyway, until her father . . .' It was pointless to continue; he barely seemed to listen. 'I've got to go now. Will you take the keys back to the office?'

He did not move. 'You know the young lady?'

'Yes.'

The black pupils in the yellow eyes pinned her. 'You know her well?'

Stella nodded, and the eyes moved slowly away from her to focus on the picture above her head.

'It is unusual,' he said.

Stella took a sideways step, as much to let him see the cabinet as to hint that he should let her leave, but he remained where he was.

'Almost everything in the picture is there,' she said, hoping to encourage him to come forward so that she could edge nearer the door. The little room, that had been chilly, now seemed to have a coldness that made breathing difficult.

'But not quite everything.' There seemed to be the suspicion of a smile in the slot of his mouth and at last he began to move towards the cabinet.

'No, not everything.' She said it merely to agree but he turned on her.

'Really?'

His intensity made her panic. 'There are other things,' she said.

'Such as?'

She did not know how to answer. Sandy had hinted at mysteries in the picture, but had seemed to understand very little herself. Stella tore her eyes from the yellow glare and looked for help in the picture itself. Potter Waterfall was seated in a high-backed chair that was almost a throne. 'They've got that,' she lied. 'They've got the chair. But it's too big to fit in here. That's what Sandy says. She's their daughter.'

She risked looking at him, despising the lie and the betrayal of Sandy but still full of fear. His attention was on the picture.

'I haven't seen it,' she said, seeking to protect herself. 'But it must be worth a lot of money.'

'You are not mistaken.' He still did not look at her and her courage began to return.

'They won't sell it,' she said. 'I know that.' She wanted to prevent him asking about it at the house. 'They don't need to sell it. They've got plenty of money, or else they wouldn't have given away all these things.'

She stopped. She had gone too far. She was revealing her own jealousy, but at least it helped to deaden the pangs of her lie. She continued to speak, deepening the envy in her voice. 'They've got everything anybody could want. They're not like the rest of us. I don't suppose they'd ever even bother to admit they've got that chair; none of our business.'

The attempt to turn him away was so blatant that she felt her paleness intensify and she waited for the harsh question that would force her to reveal her deception. The yellow eyes did not leave her, but instead of speaking he reached into an inside pocket and withdrew a slim, black wallet. There was a barely perceptible change in the set lines of his face. She saw with relief that something she had said satisfied him.

'We have something in common, Miss . . .'

She told him her name.

'Miss Grey. We are aware of value when we see it.'
He took a card from the wallet and handed it to her.
'My card will show you why.'

It was not necessary for her to look at it, but she
did so and nodded.

'You clearly have a keen eye, Miss Grey, for the
kind of article that interests me. You may be able to
lead me to something at some time.'

'They won't sell,' she said. 'It's a waste of time
asking. And I don't want them to find out who told
you.'

'Fear not, Miss Grey. The chair barely interests me.'
Yet something like triumph danced in the yellow glare.
'They have every right to keep that which belongs to
them. But I am not here to bargain. Not today.'

He paused, but he clearly had more to say. She
waited.

'I am nearing the end of a long trail; a very long
trail.' The granite face had altered, was almost
animated, flickering with gleams of a ravenous
satisfaction that made her flesh shrink. 'That picture
tells everything – the whole story – for those who can
read it.' His eyes slid upwards to the portrait and then
returned to her. 'Silas Waterfall was a seeker after
power, Miss Grey. Power of a very special sort. And
his portrait reveals it.'

His eyes returned to the bearded old man, and more
than ever Stella longed to get away. She spoke only in
order to quell the panic that again threatened her. 'I
don't know anything about that,' she said.

'Few do.' The eyes came back to her and lingered
in the silence that he let grow. Then he said, 'Silas
Waterfall was a man of science, Miss Grey. I am a
dealer in antiquities. It is the relics of his studies that
I seek.'

She nodded, humouring him.

'I have been on the verge of possessing an object, trivial in itself, that was at the heart of his experiments. Yet I was denied it – an accident intervened; at least it will be seen as an accident, but the fact that it occurred is proof to me that what I sought was almost mine; that a decision in my favour had been made.' His voice had risen, but he calmed it. He attempted a smile. 'This is nothing to you, young lady. You wonder why I even tell you. It is because I may need your assistance.'

'I don't see how,' she began.

'You have knowledge, Miss Grey, of places and people. You may be of use.' Before she could say more, he had turned to look once more at the picture, and when he spoke it was as though his words were intended for the portrait itself. 'I am here to claim that which, by right of long search, already belongs to me. A trick plucked it from me once. It shall not happen again.'

His mouth shut tight. Suddenly he gave her a stiff nod, replaced his hat and walked quickly out into the alley.

12

Sandy had run ahead without waiting and was long out of sight when Bran came down from the hill towards the house. The wooden universe was constructing itself around him again, dimming his vision, and even the sun did not warm him.

He let himself into the conservatory and sat down on a white slatted seat in the indoor garden. No sound reached him except for the distant song of a blackbird which bubbled up somewhere on the hill and was then obliterated. Above him the white ribs of the conservatory supported a film of green and silver glass, and around him heavy leaves made sluggish curves and huge flowers hung out trumpets that blared without sound. He was in the heart of an enormous still wave, held in a frozen undertow. He closed his eyes and dizziness swayed him like deep water.

'So there you are. Alone and palely loitering.'

For a moment it was his father quoting to him. He kept his eyes shut, preserving the illusion.

'I'm sorry.' Richard Ramsey had come in swiftly and silently from the house, but now stood poised on the threshold ready to retreat. He was already moving back when Bran opened his eyes.

'I didn't mean to creep up on you unawares,' said his uncle and, making excuses for his own presence in his own house, raised an arm to point at the vine that spread beneath the glass. 'It's all this foliage; it deadens the sound. And now I have disturbed your peace. I'll just fade silently away.'

He was smiling, the wren's wing eyebrows flickering, as he backed away, but Bran got to his feet.

'I was just going,' he said, apologetic himself.

'Ah.' Richard Ramsey advanced a step, and now there was, because of his shyness, an awkward confrontation. He was a man who was a mixture of ages and attitudes, grey-haired but slim-hipped enough to wear jeans without it seeming incongruous, liable to stoop with the appearance of fragility whereas he was, in fact, brown and wiry, with large, strong hands. He had a long face deeply lined with what seemed a rooted pessimism, yet when he smiled, as now, his expression was boyish and mischievous. His daughter found him full of exasperating uncertainties, and these he was displaying as he waited for Bran to break the impasse.

Bran spoke at random. 'I was looking for Sandy. We've been climbing the hill together.'

'Ah.' The wren's wings flew apart, but his expression was vague.

'She has eluded me.'

'Quite so, Bernard.' Richard Ramsey could never bring himself to call Bran by any other name, yet at the same time he made the formality a sign of friendliness, as though the name carried a respect that its shortened form lacked. 'She frequently eludes me, too.'

He smiled and Bran smiled back. They stood facing each other as though nothing would occur to make them move, and Bran once again recognized the impossibility of finding the correct way of addressing this man who was his uncle yet stood on no ceremony as regards himself. It was Richard Ramsey who broke the silence.

74

'Sit down, Bernard, sit down. I was, as a matter of fact, looking for you.'

Bran retreated to a white iron garden bench that was surrounded, almost submerged, in thick-leaved plants. Two paces away from him the man leant against a white iron table and then, realizing that this could appear to be an attempt at superiority, pulled out a chair and also sat down. There was a moment of great awkwardness, neither looking at the other, until suddenly Richard Ramsey swept both arms down to rest his elbows on his knees, bowed his head towards the floor only to raise it swiftly and gaze with sudden intensity at Bran.

'We want you here, Bernard. You know that.'

'Yes.' Bran nodded. 'Thank you.'

'Really want you.' The eyes were piercing now, desperately sincere. 'You must not think of leaving. This is your home.'

Bran could not reply, nor could he look away. His uncle . . . Richard Ramsey . . . Richard. Soon it would be merely Richard, unless he resisted it. Intimacy was being forced on him with a kindliness that was suddenly domineering. He found his mind ungratefully seeking for escape, an alternative, somewhere else to live. But there was nowhere. He must accept what was so generously offered. At length he nodded.

'Good.' The eyes released him. 'Now to business.' Richard Ramsey straightened, reached for one of the two breast pockets in his thick blue working shirt and took out a long buff envelope. 'The house has been sold. Your house, Bernard.' He believed he was being brutal even to mention such matters. 'Here.' He took out a paper and handed it over, keeping his eyes turned down to the empty envelope. 'The sale went through quite smoothly. It made a good price as you can see.'

Bran took the paper, but as he did so Richard Ramsey's head came up nervously. 'Disregard the item down there for solicitor's fees and all the rest. Ridiculous amounts. We shall pay them.' Bran opened his mouth to say something but was cut off. 'No, no, no. We would be hurt if you refused.'

The document revealed nothing. Bran could not believe that this handful of papers was all that remained; everything reduced to this. He heard himself saying, 'Has it all gone? All of it?'

'Except those things you wanted, Bernard.' Richard Ramsey uncrossed his legs and crossed them again. 'There are two sales set down there. The house and the furniture. You'll see it all.'

Bran looked down but made no attempt to study it. His mind reached out to the house as it was. But it would not hold. The certainty slid away. In his last days there, when they had allowed him inside for necessities but had taken him away at nights to sleep somewhere else, it had already begun to be unreal. For two days the clothes his mother and father had taken off when they had changed to go out lay where they had left them, his mother's dress folded neatly on the bed, his father's jacket and trousers squatting on a chair – shrunken skins. Empty. Dwarfs both, to leave so little. Yet the space they had occupied yawned on every side. He lifted his head, not believing the emptiness.

'I kept back several things you didn't mention,' said his uncle. 'All their valuables, of course, and personal things like books and papers. I thought that eventually . . .' His voice trailed away, deliberately allowing the matter to subside.

Vaguely, Bran brought his eyes around to rest on the worried face.

'I'm terribly sorry, Bernard, to have to bring it all back.' He was in anguish.

'No,' said Bran. 'It doesn't matter.'

Nothing mattered. There was nothing more to say. They were trapped in a silence so rigid that even though both heard the door open and someone step into the conservatory neither of them turned.

'Conference?'

It was Sandy's voice and suddenly her father laughed, relieved.

'You might say,' he said.

'What about?' She advanced on them. 'Me?'

The eyebrows were lifted high, and turned towards Bran. 'Have you ever come across a conceit like my daughter's?'

She, basking as always in his approval, turned his unmeant question into a real one.

'Am I,' she said to Bran, 'conceited, as my father says?'

He did not answer and she came a step nearer.

'Well?' She was very close now and he could almost feel her warmth. He began to smile. 'Well?' she repeated. 'What do you think of me? Am I conceited?'

'No more than you have cause to be,' he said, and her father laughed.

'Very funny,' she said.

'You were being flattered, my dear,' said Richard Ramsey.

'I'd prefer not to be flattered by somebody with wet trouser legs.'

There were going to be embarrassing explanations of the hilltop encounter, and to forestall them Bran held up the document. 'I've just been given this.'

'Is it serious?' she said. 'You look as though you've just failed an exam or something.'

There was no antagonism in the way she spoke, but her father feared her tactlessness and broke in. 'I was just telling him that the house is sold.'

'Oh yes. I heard about that.' She was interested. 'You're quite well off now.'

'Sandy!' The wren's wings were jammed close together in a show of anger, but no more than a show, and she was unperturbed.

'Well it's true.' She sat down on the bench alongside Bran. 'You're a man of property now.'

Her father was fidgeting, and his ignored ferocity drained off. 'Pay no attention to her, Bernard.'

'Bernard!' She laughed. 'Do I have to call him that, now he's rich? And you are rich, aren't you, Bran-tub?'

Her father lifted his head, and Bran was suddenly aware that, for the first time, Richard Ramsey was regarding his daughter and Bran himself as a pair, a possible pair, and was pleased, giving them his blessing. But it was too simple; too much could happen. Bran could not acknowledge what was in the man's mind and turned away.

'I'll take you out somewhere,' he said to Sandy. 'I can afford it.'

'I love rich men. It's going to cost you a lot.' She twisted towards her father. 'Isn't he nice?' she said. 'Nice and rich.'

At that moment, somewhere deep within the house, the old-fashioned doorbell jangled on its spring and danced uncertainly into silence. It was Bran's cue to escape.

'I'd better get out of these wet things,' he said and began to move towards the door, but before he got there it opened and Martha Ramsey stood there. She was flustered. Her large dark eyes, full of apprehension, sought her husband.

'There's somebody to see you,' she said. 'I've put him in your office.'

Richard Ramsey got to his feet. 'Who is it?'

'You know.' She was willing him to understand without having to say the name aloud. 'He's come back.'

Bran saw it was something she wanted to keep private and edged towards the door.

'Who?' said her husband innocently, and Sandy laughed at his obtuseness.

She advanced on him 'You know,' she said. 'Lovely little sharp teeth.'

Understanding dawned, and most of the pleasure left his face. 'I suppose I'd better see him.'

Richard Ramsey moved past his wife who hesitated, began to follow him, and then changed her mind.

'Off you go, Mother.' Sandy began to usher her out. 'You know you want to be there.'

'It might be private.'

'You know it isn't.'

Without any more persuading Martha Ramsey left, and Sandy faced Bran.

'They're both the same,' she said. 'Without me to tell them what to do sometimes they'd dither for ever.'

Vaguely, he thought she wanted to be alone with him, but now she began to bustle him.

'You need to change. You'll catch your death.'

'I shouldn't think so.'

'Yes you will. You're soaked.'

'But that's not what you're worried about.'

'Yes I am, Bran.'

'No. You're trying to get rid of me, too. Why?'

'Because you're wet and horrible.'

'But rich.' He tried to divert her.

'That too.' She humoured him and at the same

time began pulling him towards the door. 'Away you go.' He tried to kiss her but she avoided him. 'No. I've got something I must do.'

'Secret?'

'No.'

'Tell me.'

'Later. Perhaps.'

'Promise?'

She sighed once, quickly, and made up her mind. She stepped right up to him and put her arms around his waist, pulling him close. Then she put her mouth on his and let him know that her passion was still there.

'There,' she said, 'is that promise enough?'

'I think so.'

'It will have to do.' She pushed him away. 'Now off you go. Quickly.'

13

Bran changed and came out on to the landing carrying his wet things. He was barefoot, for the foolish reason that he had been unable to find any dry socks. Now he felt more than foolish; his search for socks was bound to be troublesome to others and would emphasize the fact that he was an interloper. He hesitated on the dark, uneven boards outside his room, took a step forward, changed his mind, and decided to make one final search. He was stooping to lay his wet clothes on the carpet so as not to mark the polish of the boards when a door opened in the hall and he heard voices.

'Have you got rid of him?'

'Yes, Martha. He's gone.'

His aunt sighed. 'Oh!' she said, 'you've no idea of the relief. I can't stand to have him anywhere near me.'

He heard the rustle of her dress and the door close and he breathed again. He had almost, to add to his other crimes, become an eavesdropper. Then, with a jolt, he heard them speak again. They had not left the hall. It was as though a double trap had sprung on him, fixing him where he was crouched.

'I should have told the boy, Martha. I should have had him in and told him. It's his affair, not ours.'

'Richard.' She was coaxing him. 'You did the right thing. How could he have faced that horrible man? How could he, after all he's been through?'

'I'll have to tell him.'

'Yes, my dear. But later; not now.'

Silence again, and he guessed they had their arms around each other. They were embracing while he, who had no place in the house, clung to the carpet above them. He raised his head, hoping they were out of sight beneath him, but through the heavy balustrade he saw Richard Ramsey's grey hair and the blue shoulder of his shirt against which his wife rested her head. He could not move. He crouched lower until he was again out of sight and tried to breathe quietly in the apple-scented air drifting down from the lofts.

Then his aunt's voice again. 'I can't believe Alice told that man so much. I can't believe it.'

'He knew all about it, Martha. He knew it existed, and he's prepared to pay. I think I believe him.'

'A man like that!'

Her husband drew in his breath to answer but before he could do so there were footsteps from the back of the house and Sandy was there. Her voice was loud.

'I saw him,' she said. 'I was out in the garden. He doesn't give up very easily, does he?'

'He's gone,' said her mother, 'and he won't be coming back.'

'Pity. I still think he's sweet, but I wouldn't trust him an inch.'

Her father laughed, and she said, 'Well it's true; you don't have to trust everybody you like. We're not all like you, you know, leaving your safe wide open, telling everybody everything. I'm jolly glad we've got that hiding place.'

'Very well, my daughter.' He was chuckling still. 'If that's the way you feel about my security arrangements . . .'

'Security arrangements!'

'If that's the way you feel, there's something else that should be put in your hiding place.'

'Richard!' His wife interrupted, but it was too late.

'She ought to know about it, my dear. And even *I* think she might be right about the safe. We've got to be careful.'

As he spoke he was already moving them out of the hall. Bran heard Sandy say, 'If it's something to do with that thing, shouldn't we tell Bran about it?' But a door closed behind them before he heard what they decided. He waited, but they did not come back.

Griff, keeping his chin tucked behind his shoulder, danced in and let go a left and right. His fists smacked the punchbag and motes of dust sprang from the split seam to spin in a bar of sunlight. He sidestepped into the sun himself and threw a left. His timing was right and the heavy bag lurched. That was it. Watchfully, as though it was a man tottering in front of him, he backed away, not letting his arms fall until he was out of reach, and then went to the door of the shed. He was sweating and breathing heavily.

His father, coming down the path from the back of the Black Swan, stopped when he saw him and jerked his head. 'He wants you.' He turned and began to walk back.

Unlacing the gloves with his teeth, Griff followed. He was big, almost as large as his father whose broad back was rolling ahead of him.

'What does he want?'

'You better see.' The publican did not look round. 'He don't seem too happy.'

'He better not try anything with me.'

His father grunted and turned aside into the bar where he was getting ready for opening time, and

Griff continued along the passage to the front parlour.

Harman was staring out through the thickly-leaded window into the square. Griff stopped a half-pace inside the door, still breathing heavily, and removed his gloves. He slapped them together and waited. Harman did not move, and Griff wiped his forehead on his arm and sighed.

'I heard you, boy.'

Griff lowered his arm slowly. His fleshy face was wary and had become sullen, almost shifty. 'What do you want?' he said.

His tone brought Harman round with a jerk. His mouth was open to bark, but then his eyes took in the gloves and Griff's perspiring face and his anger was checked. Griff was satisfied; he had established that he was not to be trifled with. But when the man spoke his tone was unimpressed.

'Fetch my bag. I am leaving.'

Griff, taking his time, began to tie the laces of his gloves together. 'Now?'

Harman's jaw hardened. 'If you please.'

Griff turned away.

'How old are you, boy?'

He took his time turning around to face the man and let his insolence show. He was enjoying himself. 'Seventeen.'

'And I am sixty.'

Griff shrugged. It was nothing to him.

'And I do not train my muscles.'

Griff waited. The old fool could not be suggesting a contest. There was a glint of something very like amusement in the man's face.

'So why is it that you are obeying my orders?'

'I don't have to.'

'But you will. Because I will pay you.' He paused,

his yellow eyes glittering on Griff. 'So which is the more powerful; your muscle or this?' The hand in his pocket jingled silver.

'There ain't no comparison. They've got nothing to do with each other.'

'You are proud, young man. You have the pride of your father.'

Griff knew what he was talking about. His father had told him of his refusal to sell anything to the visitor. 'My father's right,' he said.

'Even pride has a price. I could buy this whole inn at a price your father could not refuse. Now please fetch my bag.' He turned back to the window, his point won.

'You're wrong,' said Griff. 'He wouldn't sell if he didn't want to.'

Harman made a slight, dismissive movement with his hand and Griff was angered. 'You couldn't have it because it ain't his to sell.'

The man looked over his shoulder. 'Then I could buy it over his head. Now please go.'

'You'd never get it.'

Harman was looking out of the window. 'My bag, please.'

'Because it belongs to somebody who don't need your money.' There was no movement from the man. He had done with the childishness of the argument. But Griff had to press the point home. 'It belongs to them you've just been to see up the hill. They'd never sell. I know that.'

His success was startling. Harman spun round. The flesh of his face was grainy, as hard as stone. 'They own this?' The words made one brief, grating sound.

'They own everything.'

'And claim that which is not theirs!' Anger brought

out a slab of fact that was none of Griff's business. The mouth shut.

'I don't know about that, but I know you'd never get this place.' Griff did not try to keep triumph out of his voice. He looked at the smaller, older man with something like pity and then made up his mind to be magnanimous.

'If you give me your car keys I'll take your bag to it.'

He held out his hand but the man, instead of giving him the keys, grasped it. 'You are pleased with yourself, young man. You have won the argument.'

Griff reddened. He had not expected a reconciliation like this. 'That's all right.' He relaxed his grip, preparing to break away, but Harman held him.

'There is a wide difference in our ages,' said the man, and Griff nodded. 'And I have not been in training.'

Harman looked up at him and his grip did not lessen. Gradually, Griff tightened his own fingers to match the pressure. It was a hint. If he was not released, Harman would learn what training had enabled him to do. It had no effect. Right; he must be taught a lesson. Griff let all the power of his arm surge into his fingers. Something moved, and he was terrified. The old bones were cracking inside his grasp. He opened his mouth about to apologize when pain shot up his own arm. His own grip was nothing. His fingers had straightened and his own bones were grinding one against another.

The man did not seem to have moved a muscle. His mouth was a dead straight line and his eyes which, until then, had been the frightening thing about him, were fixed, expressionless. It was as though the power in the man had been switched to another outlet.

86

The pain pierced every joint, and unwilling words came out of Griff's mouth. 'No,' he said. 'No.'

And then Harman released him, turning away to dig into his pocket to put first the key and then a small pile of silver on the nearest table.

Griff, pale, watched him but was ignored. Without even glancing once more towards him, Harman walked back the few paces he had moved from the window and resumed his contemplation of the square.

In the soft light and quietness, Bran crossed his room and sat in the deep window-ledge. They had secrets from him. They offered him their home but he would never be part of it.

Below him the conservatory roof sloped away, slightly dusty like the still surface of a pond, and beneath the glass the vine spread like a water plant. His vision slid lazily down through layers of light and shade, and it was with no curiosity at all, fish-like and vacant, that he saw the foreshortened figures of Sandy and her parents moving like water creatures over the bottom of the pond.

They came out from under the vine leaves and crossed the flagstones to where a sundial stood on a stone pedestal. It occurred to him that it must be there as an ornament for only rarely could the sun penetrate the foliage to fall directly on it, but they gathered as though they were consulting it. Sandy was plainly the instigator for it was she who approached it most closely, stooping right over its dial, senselessly putting her own shadow over that of the gnomon. She even grasped the pedestal at the edges of the sundial's face, and then he saw her sway as she tugged at it.

It moved with a jerk but he could not see properly what happened next because all three crouched and hid whatever it was they were examining at the pedestal's base. After a moment her father went away, back under the vine leaves into the house, and they crouched where they were until he returned. He was carrying something, but his shoulders and arms obscured it from Bran's view and he put it down on the floor in front of his wife.

There was a long, tense moment during which nobody moved, and then Sandy's head tilted as though she was reaching for something that lay between the three of them and then he thought he heard a little shriek followed by laughter. A moment later they stood up.

Sandy shook back her hair, raising her face, and looked straight at him. Instinctively he drew back and lost sight of them under the leaves. He anticipated a shout but none came, and he realized that the two layers of glass made by the roof and his window had probably made him no more than a blur to her, but he waited before he advanced his head again. He thought he heard stone grate on stone but the sound ceased before the sundial came in view again. It stood where it had been before, and they had gone.

14

Stella had finished the housework and was reading when the knock came at the front door. It would be Mr Ramsey, Sandy's father. Of all the people in the village only he would be so formal as not to come to the back of the house. He was their landlord, and it was because of that that he took no liberties.

She liked him, but in an uncertain way because both were made awkward by the gulf between them, and as she went through the tiny front room to open the door for him she despised herself for straightening her dress and tidying a cushion. The last thing he would do would be to make an inspection, and the last thing she would do would be to invite him to do so.

'Miss Grey.' Harman, outlined against the flowers that crowded the narrow garden, stood like an incongruous grey statue with his hat raised a polite inch. 'I'm afraid I startled you.'

Stella quickly recovered. 'Won't you come in?'

He went by her into the room and paused but she, as she would have done with Richard Ramsey, directed him into the little room at the back. She removed her book from the arm of the chair. 'Will you sit down?'

'You will guess why I called, Miss Grey.' He remained standing. 'You will have seen from my card that my business is to buy things. I wish to buy something from you.'

It was so curtly said, so surprising, that for a long moment she faced him across the table, unable to gather her thoughts. But she knew she must not be intimidated.

'I think you have come to the wrong house,' she said. 'We have nothing down here worth selling.'

His face gleamed for an instant as though he approved of her defiance. Then he said, 'You are mistaken.'

His eyes left her and he began to inspect the room, as calmly as if he had been invited in for that purpose, as though it was a museum. She began to resent him.

She followed his gaze towards the high mantle of the fireplace. A photograph of her mother stood there in an oval pewter frame, and Stella jerked her head round, about to refuse him, making it an excuse to show him he was unwelcome, but he inclined his forehead once more to indicate that it was not the photograph or the frame that interested him. It was something at the end of the mantle.

'That's an old toffee tin,' she said. 'We use it as a tea caddy.'

It had a hinged lid and fluted corners and was decorated with a pattern of bright blue birds swooping through and perched among golden tendrils and leaves. Despite its age, the birds and gilded foliage were bright, barely marked even at the corners. Her mother had loved it, and so did she.

'I would give you fifteen pounds for that.'

She laughed, disbelieving.

'I would sell it for thirty,' he said.

It was a confrontation, but with mercantile honesty put forward as a bond of good faith. She gave a half-smile, letting him know she appreciated what was happening, but rebuffed him.

'Not for sale; it's an heirloom.'

'It was merely an example.'

She spoke quickly. 'I think you'd better come back later. When my father gets home from work.'

He bowed slightly. 'Quite so. Some other time, Miss Grey.'

She was relieved and drew in her breath preparing to lead him to the door. But he did not move.

She watched him. A smile on that face was barely more detectable than a shadow that deepens or diminishes in a slight change of light, but he seemed amused, grimly. 'There is a conspiracy afoot, Miss Grey, to prevent me from removing anything from this village. Even a tin canister once given away with toffees is denied me.' He paused.

'I'm sorry,' she said.

'I do not complain. People have every right to retain what is theirs.' The small eyes held her; she could see him thinking ahead. When he spoke again it was to change the subject. 'Chance operates in a mysterious way. Without our chance meeting in the museum I should not have known whom to approach. I need an agent.'

The last words were snapped out like a challenge and she had no reply. He did not seem to expect one, for he kept silent only long enough for the idea to be received.

'I hinted as much at our previous meeting, Miss Grey. It cannot be a surprise to you. We have similar interests. I was impressed by your knowledge of that little display.'

'There are other people who know much more.'

He raised a hand. 'Perhaps. But I have made a decision.' The gesture of the raised hand was so peremptory it was almost comic, but it silenced her.

Once again he seemed to change the subject. 'This cottage, unless I am much mistaken, does not belong to your father.'

It was none of Harman's business. She did not reply.

'He would rent it, I imagine, from the family on the hill.'

'As a matter of fact he does.' She let her antagonism show.

'They seem to own most things.' His eyes were very sharp, as though he expected to detect jealousy.

'I suppose they do.' She shrugged.

'I have seen the young lady of the house. She has the air of ownership; as though the whole village were hers.'

'She's a friend of mine.' Stella attempted to be haughty, cutting off what seemed an invitation to agree with him.

'I had imagined so,' he said blandly. 'There cannot be too many people of your age within a reasonable distance. A newcomer must be welcome.'

He waited for an answer. They both knew to whom he referred.

'I haven't even met him,' she said.

'But you will.' He turned away. Whatever his reason for mentioning the tragic, shrouded figure who had come to live on the hill, the subject had been dropped.

She watched him as he reached inside his jacket and brought out the slim wallet from which, at their previous meeting, he had taken his card.

'An agent, Miss Grey, must have a retainer.'

His hand went to his wallet and a sheaf of new pound notes lay on the table. 'Twenty,' he said. 'You will soon learn my requirements. You have clever eyes.' His short, square-tipped fingers were touching

92

the money, tapping and caressing, making the smooth new paper slide and flicker, fan out and come together, faster and faster until it was pulsating like the wing-beats of some huge green and white insect. It was a conjuror's trick, but Stella shuddered. An instant more and he would make it fly, rise from the table and flap obscenely towards her. Unless she ignored it; let him see that childishness like this would not win her.

She dragged her eyes from the flickering money, lifting her chin, and gazed at him squarely. The yellow glare that met her was anonymous, as in-different as the tawny stare of a caged lion looking beyond the crowds towards a remembered prospect of Africa. The yellowness, she saw, was flecked with brown, and the flecks were not stationary, but swam in his eyes' fluid, moving like small creatures over the face of a desert, creeping on the baking sands, ex-hausted, wilting, tired beyond any wish to survive. She saw them become sluggish and sink, merge with their shadows, sink in the yellow sand.

'. . . nineteen, twenty,' said Harman, and she realized that she had not been listening as he had been counting the money. 'And there will, of course, be a commission for you on anything I decide to buy.'

He was making for the door, the matter settled, and she was following. But she was still thinking it over. There could be no objection to doing what he asked, it would harm nobody; yet the money was too much. She searched her mind for questions to put to him, but he was at the front door and on the doorstep before anything occurred to her.

'If I do it,' she said, 'am I allowed to tell anybody?'

He bowed slightly as he replaced his hat. 'That is entirely your affair, Miss Grey. You must do this task as you think fit.' There was an utter lack of expression in his face. 'The retainer, of course, is payable each month we are in business together.'

And he was gone, moving carefully down the path between the flowers.

Stella closed the door and went through to the back room. The money had been left in a fan, easily countable. She stood looking down at it. He did not ask for much. There could be nothing wrong in letting him know what there was in the village. It would even be enjoyable, a test, to see if she could think in his terms.

She reached for the money, but before her fingers touched it she held back. There must be more to it than he had said; so much money was not handed over for so little. But he had offered almost as much for an old toffee tin, and said he could make as much again in profit. He knew where he could dip into running rivers of money; he had that power. And to be near him was to feel the surge of it. For the excitement alone it was worth it. And nothing would be lost; nothing compromised.

Stella knew that, even before she began arguing with herself, her mind had been made up. Swiftly, she folded in the fan of money, stacked it and, crushing it in her hand, went upstairs to hide it.

15

They had long disappeared from the conservatory below his window and all was quiet in the house when, for the second time, Bran left his room. There was nobody in the hall and he went down, seeking dry clothes. He was still barefoot and could not help moving silently along the short, dark passage that led from the hall to the kitchen, when once more, and again unwillingly, he heard voices. The kitchen door was ajar as though the house itself, surreptitiously, was determined to offer up the secrets of its occupants. He halted, about to take himself out of earshot, when Sandy raised her voice.

'Leave it to me,' she said. 'I can talk to him better than you.'

Then her mother. 'No, Sandy.'

'You don't sound as though you trust me.'

'That's a silly thing to say.' But there was doubt in her mother's voice, and after a moment she added, 'It's just that I don't want you leading him on, or anything like that.'

'Leading him on?' Laughter bubbled up in Sandy's voice. 'What do you mean, Mother?'

'You know very well what I mean, so don't do it.'

Bran could almost see Martha Ramsey blushing, and under cover of her daughter's loud laughter he began to retreat. But not fast enough. He heard footsteps crossing the kitchen as though heading for the corridor and he had no choice but to go forward. He pushed open the door and went in. Sandy was standing just inside by the dresser, and Martha Ramsey was at the long, low window setting places for lunch. She looked up, startled.

'Oh, Bran! How long have you been there?'

'I'm looking for some dry socks.' He entered as though that alone was on his mind. Sandy was reaching down plates and would not have gone into the corridor. He could easily have made his escape.

'We were just talking about you,' she said.

'Dry socks.' Her mother interrupted. 'Get the boy some. Over there. Look.' There was a pile of ironing on a chair.

'Help yourself,' said Sandy.

He turned to his aunt, holding up his wet things. 'I'm sorry about these. If you can tell me where I can hang them . . .'

'Don't you worry about them.' She cut short his apology. 'It's not your fault. I know who led you into it. She's responsible.'

'Thank you very much.' Sandy was sarcastic, but her mother ignored her, bustling about, deliberately getting Bran to assist her so that Sandy was effectively silenced. She watched them, waiting her turn, and eventually, when dry socks had been found and he had put them on, and then his shoes, and he was standing up, tightening his belt, she looked him up and down. He had shed his grey, and was wearing a striped blue and white shirt, and jeans.

'That's better,' she said.

'Yes,' said her mother. 'It's uncomfortable walking about in bare feet.'

'I mean his clothes. He looks fit to be with.'

Martha Ramsey gave a little grimace towards him.

'I hope your girlfriend doesn't talk to you like this, Bran.'

'There isn't one,' said Sandy. 'He told me.'

'Well it won't be long before there is.'

'My mother thinks you're a good-looker.' Sandy, with a situation to exploit, was pleased. 'You know what she likes about you best? Your lovely blond hair. And then that square sort of chin you've got. She says you ought to be in advertisements.'

'You're embarrassing the boy. Leave him alone.'

'But what I like about you most of all,' she said, facing him, 'is that you're rich.'

Martha Ramsey sighed heavily. 'That's my daughter. She embarrasses everybody all the time.'

'He's taking me out this afternoon, aren't you, Bran?'

He looked towards her mother, raising his eyebrows. 'It's the first I've heard about it,' he said.

Sandy accused him. 'You promised.'

'Don't let her bully you,' said her mother.

'I won't.' But he guessed that arrangements had already been made.

Late in the afternoon, walking down the hill through the trees, she said, 'Actually it was my mother's idea that we should get out of the house. She thinks it will be good for you.'

'It certainly didn't sound like that. Where am I taking you?'

They were passing the lock-keeper's cottage and she was gazing at it beyond the high hollyhocks at the gate and did not seem to hear him.

'Good,' she said, 'nobody about,' and she quickened her pace as though pleased to get by unseen.

'Who lives there?' he asked.

D

'Only Stella. My best friend, but I don't want her playing gooseberry.'

'I thought we were going out to meet people.'

'Oh we are.' She looked at him out of the corner of her eye. 'It's going to be a giddy whirl. But we don't have to be in a hurry to invite everybody.'

They crossed the lock gates to where the tall buildings of the pottery loomed over the water. There was a faint hum of machinery from somewhere, but even that died away as they walked past and followed the short road to enter the square. It lay open to the sun of the late afternoon, deserted, dried out and glaring except where the grove like a sleeping cat huddled a patch of shadow beneath it. Under its branches, where their footfalls were deadened by the dust, Bran paused. He turned his head to look along the length of the square. The columns of the Assembly Rooms guarded one end, and at the other the shallow flight of steps led down to the water and the tall trees on the other side. The house fronts made a wall on either side.

'This is all new,' he said.

'Old. Ages old.'

'New to me. I've never been here before.'

'Of course you have. When you were small.'

He searched for a memory, but all that remained was a kind of dream.

'But there's nobody about,' he said. 'Not a soul moving.'

'There will be, later.' She led him out of the grove to where a striped blind, like a half-lowered eyelid, shaded the front of a tiny shop. Two round tables with three or four chairs to each stood on the pavement and she sat down, in the shade but with her legs thrust out into the sun.

'This is it,' she said. 'The Savoy Tea Rooms.'

The shop had two bow-windows, each with small panes, that stood on either side of the door. Bran looked up at the nameboard. 'It says Simpson and Son.'

'The Savoy. Where you promised to entertain me. Bring me the menu.'

He looked at the tables and even peered through the dim panes but saw nothing that looked like a menu.

'There isn't one.'

'I know that, stupid.'

He sat down at the other side of her table. 'There must be some mistake.'

'Oh?'

'I came here to have tea with a young lady.'

'Well?'

'There's no menu.' He paused. 'And no young lady, either.'

Coyly, she rested her chin in her palm. 'What a pity.'

'So may I offer *you* some refreshment?' he asked.

'How kind.'

'Alas, there is no means of telling what they have.'

She turned towards him. 'Look into my eyes.'

He did so.

'If there is no menu,' she said, 'hadn't you better go inside and see what there is?'

He stood up and went to the door, craning his neck to see into the dim interior.

'There's ice cream,' he said over his shoulder.

'Ice cream!' She turned her eyes heavenwards in despair.

'There's Coke.'

'I'm hungry.'

'Cucumber sandwiches?'

'Very nice,' she said primly.

'And buttered scones?'

'Lovely. Get me both.'

'They haven't got either.'

He walked into the shop without giving her a chance to reply and came back with two bags of crisps and two bottles with straws in them.

'You're trying to turn a girl's head,' she said. 'I suppose you think I won't be able to refuse you anything after this.'

He sat down, smiling, and turned away to look across the square.

'Now he's offering me his handsome profile,' she said.

'We're not alone.'

She followed his eyes. There was someone moving where the shadows were gathering in front of the houses opposite.

'That's her,' said Sandy. He caught a glimpse of a blue dress before the girl vanished behind the grove. 'She's deceitful.'

He waited for the girl to emerge but she did not reappear.

'Why do you say that?'

'Because she never tells you what she's thinking. And she's so aloof. She pretends that nothing affects her. She even says she's not interested in boys.' Sandy laughed.

'Which is impossible.'

'Typical male conceit,' she said. 'I think you might be a match for her.'

'Where has she gone now?'

'That's just it. She's sneaking along to see her Griff.'

'No restraint.' He nodded seriously. 'Not at all like you.'

She put the straw to her lips and smiled as she sucked. 'I wonder,' she said.

'Wonder what?'

'I wonder what she'll think of you now.'

'That hardly matters. She's already got a boyfriend.'

'Him? He's not her type. He's a boxer and all that; a real thickie. And she's always reading.'

'And all that,' he added, mimicking her. 'You begin to make her sound attractive.'

'Oh she is. I told you she's my best friend and I hate her.' Abruptly she changed the subject. 'But I didn't want her to come over because I've got something to tell you.'

'I know.' Her recklessness was catching. 'I heard you talking about it. In the kitchen, before lunch.'

'You sneaky little beast. I might have known. You're just the same as slithery Stella. Sly.'

'I couldn't help it. I didn't hear much. I don't even know what it's about.'

She put down the bottle and leant forward, putting her elbows on the table and resting her chin in her hands.

'You're richer than you think.'

He waited. There was a slight upturned snubness in her nose, and her lips, moist where she had been drinking, gave her a strangely animal look as though she had just lifted up her face from feeding.

'Well,' she said. 'Don't you want to know?'

'I think you are about to tell me.'

'Suppose I am. Can't you sound interested?'

'I am more interested in you.'

She was slightly taken aback, but pleased. She tilted her head and looked at him along her eyes. 'Later,' she said. 'Control yourself.'

'It's difficult.'

'It's the box.' She looked at him squarely. 'You know the one I mean. The one that belongs to you.'

He nodded. Those slightly upturned, animal nostrils would breathe out a hidden heat. He longed to touch her.

'That man who came to see my father this morning wants to buy it, but they won't let him have it.'

There were two parts to his mind, like layers of water of different temperatures. Somewhere on the surface he was chilled, listening to Harman's voice talking to his mother, persuading her to act against what she believed to be right; but beneath it, as he watched Sandy, he was bathed in warmth.

'But it's yours,' she said. 'It's not up to them.'

'I don't care.'

'I would. You know that little man would give a lot for it.'

'Perhaps it's worth more.' He was teasing her but she took him seriously.

'Do you think so?'

He shrugged. 'It might be; it's antique.'

'Oh.' She seemed disappointed. 'I thought you meant something else.'

He waited for her to continue but she avoided his eye and he himself had to say it. 'Something to do with alchemy,' he said. 'Making gold.'

She coloured. 'That's stupid.'

'But it's what was in your mind.'

'Well if he believed it, that would make him want it. And it would be a good idea for you to get rid of it while he was still greedy – before he came to his senses and realized it was all stupidity!'

He gazed at her without speaking.

'Don't look at me like that,' she said.

'I can't help it.' Then, because it was easy now to

disconcert her, he said, 'That was why, when the visitor came this morning, you wanted to be rid of me so quickly, wasn't it? So you could go and listen outside the door.'

Her eyes almost left his. 'I needn't have bothered. They told me all about it later. They always do.'

'Not very co-operative of them to have no secrets for you to find out.'

She pulled down the corners of her mouth. 'They're so pure.'

'But I'm not. I have secrets. And so have you.'

'Not any more. I've told you everything.'

'Have you?' He gazed at her steadily and after a while she raised her eyebrows and shrugged. She was about to turn away when he spoke slowly. 'The sundial covers a secret.'

Her eyes and mouth opened wide together.

'When I was in my room I looked down and saw you.'

Her smile was suddenly wide. She put out her hand, twinkling her fingers in the excited, impatient gesture he recognized, and made him get to his feet. 'Come on, Brandywine, it's time to reveal all.'

16

They did not make it. Sandy was just about to open the first of the two glass doors leading from the hall to the conservatory when, in the dark corner under the stairs, the door of her father's study opened.

'Damn!' she said under her breath, and pulled up short so that Bran almost collided with her. It was all done so guiltily that he tensed, expecting suspicion, but her father, as she obviously expected, noticed nothing.

'You're back early,' he said mildly.

'Only for a minute. I've got to fetch something.' She tried to edge Bran away but he resisted her. He suddenly did not want to conspire against this shadowy, benign figure who smiled at them in the dim light of the hall.

'If you have a moment to spare, Bernard.'

'Bran.' His daughter, exasperated with both of them, corrected him.

Her father chuckled, and blandly refused to pander to her. He stepped back, inviting Bran to enter, but at the same time he spoke to Sandy. 'Don't let us prevent you from doing what you came for. I do not anticipate that what I have to say to Bernard will take long.'

She sighed and clicked her tongue. 'I know you and your "anticipates".' She stepped forward and entered the room ahead of them both. 'I expect we'll be here for hours.'

Bran smiled, almost apologizing for her, and Richard Ramsey allowed his eyebrows to rise as he smiled in return to show that he understood. Instantly, in those faint gestures, they showed each other a current that ran beneath the surface, and Bran knew that, from now on, everything they said could have, when they chose, an edge of meaning beyond the reach of anyone else, even Sandy. Such things happened.

Within the room the trees crowding close to the house intensified the dusk, and a shaded lamp burned on the cluttered top of the wide desk. Bran had not been here before and he realized, as he looked around himself, that this, for Richard Ramsey at least, was the heart of the house. It was partly study, partly office, but more like a library than either. The walls were entirely lined in bookcases that reached to the ceiling, and some had brass grilles like those he had seen protecting rare volumes in stately homes. There were side tables littered with papers and books in the kind of order that only the owner would comprehend, and two deep leather armchairs into which they were waved while Richard Ramsey, so that the desk should not be between them, pushed aside some of the clutter and perched on its edge, one leg swinging. The light, reflected obliquely upwards, made strong shadows on his face, but neither the close quietness of the room nor the brooding figure of her father above them impressed Sandy.

'Well?' she said.

For once her father ignored her and spoke directly to Bran. 'I am feeling a little guilty, Bernard.' He was aware of his daughter's objection to the name and raised his hand to silence her. He was speaking to whatever had not changed. 'We had a visitor earlier today who wished to see you. You ought to have been allowed to meet him, but we told you nothing because it would have been painful for you.' He paused. 'I took it upon myself to act on your behalf.'

'I know.' Bran saw from the corner of his eye that Sandy was leaning forward about to say something to cover up his eavesdropping, but he spoke too quickly for her. 'I overheard you when you were talking in the hall. I was on the landing.'

Sandy threw herself back in her chair, disgusted with him, and there was severity, for a different reason, in her father's face, but Bran made no excuses.

'I know who your visitor was, and I know why he was here. He wanted to buy the box that belonged to my mother.' The eyes above him were hidden in shadow, but he faced their emptiness and continued. 'I also know where you keep it hidden because I saw you from my window.'

He had said all he intended, and now he waited. Sandy kept a sulky silence.

'You have finished, Bernard?'

He nodded.

'You have left something out.'

'No.' Bran shook his head.

'Your motive.'

Bran remained silent.

'You do not say whether you overheard us by design or by accident.'

He was being offered a way out but he refused it. 'It doesn't matter. I heard you and I saw you. And I said nothing.'

Richard Ramsey had ceased to swing his leg. His face was a pattern of shadows, expressionless, without a trace of forgiveness. He moved forward, bringing his foot to the floor, and stood over Bran.

'In that case, Bernard,' his voice was level, speaking in judgement, 'you are a man to be trusted.' He turned away but even the negative gesture was a sign of approval. Their understanding was complete.

'I don't get you two,' said Sandy.

Her father, sitting behind the desk with the light on his face, smiled and made no attempt to reply. Instead, he reached down to a drawer, lifted something from it and put it on the corner he had cleared.

'You cheat!' Sandy cried.

The little box squatted in the full glare of the light so toad-like that at any moment it would begin to crawl towards the shadows.

'I brought it out of hiding because it is not ours to hide,' said her father.

'But I was just going to take him to show him where it was! That's what we came back for.'

Her father noticed that now she too was being truthful.

'Well I have saved you the trouble,' he said drily.

'You're hopeless!' She slumped in her seat again.

'The casket is yours, Bernard. You must do with it as you think fit.'

There was something in Richard Ramsey's voice that stirred Bran's memory. He had heard it in the hall that morning; a doubt about how he had dealt with the man who had come to buy the box.

'Do you think I should sell?'

'That is up to you, Bernard.'

He offered no advice, but Bran needed it. 'What do you think?' he asked. 'Has he some right to it?'

The eyebrows went up and came down, and when he spoke it was with reluctance. 'He says your mother had agreed to sell.'

So that was it. A promise had been made and now

it was in danger of not being honoured. Richard Ramsey had a duty to her memory and to her son, but even stronger was the desire that the box should not fall into strange hands. The dilemma tormented him.

Bran allowed himself a pause. 'She did intend to sell the box,' he said. 'That's why they went out to celebrate.'

The eyes left Bran for the first time, and the long face was weighted with sadness. 'Then it is as he said. He has a claim to it.'

'No.'

The face came up. 'But if she promised, Bernard . . .'

'She only made her mind up after he had left.'

The eyes beneath the eyebrows hovered on the brink of distrust, sensing a mere legal distinction, not a moral certainty, but Bran gazed back without flinching.

'They were never in touch again,' he said. 'She promised him nothing.'

'Is this true, Bernard?'

'Absolutely true.'

But doubt still clung. 'But he was right when he said it was her intention to sell.'

Sandy had lost her patience. 'Oh for goodness' sake! He's not entitled to it unless you're soft enough to give in !'

'Bernard?' Her father, having raised all the moral niceties, scrupulously left the decision to him.

There had been a moment when, talking of his mother, Bran's resolution had almost failed him. But he found himself smiling. He wanted to take life by the throat and give it a shake. 'It's Catch 22,' he said. 'No matter what I do I'm wrong in somebody's eyes.' There was sympathy in the man's face and also a tinge of admiration. 'So,' said Bran. 'I'm going to forget the past. It's too much of a mess.' He paused and then delivered judgement. 'The only thing that nobody has mentioned is whether it is right for that man to have the box. It isn't. That box was never intended for people like him. I know it. So I'm going to keep it from him, no matter how.'

He stopped, this time forcing some response. Richard Ramsey's smile was slow but gradually it lit the whole of his face. 'Then I'm with you, Bernard, all the way.'

'Well I'm not,' said Sandy. 'I only said you didn't have to sell it to him because I thought you could get a better price somewhere else. But I can see what's going to happen. Bran's going to be like you and give everything to a stupid museum.'

But her father was barely listening. He had put out a hand and was turning the box, reading aloud the words on its sides. 'IN TIME OF NEED'. He looked up. 'That can hardly mean anything now. I've already discovered the secret of the glaze – so, Bernard, I'm afraid I've made this into no more than an historical oddity.'

'You may think so,' Sandy got to her feet, 'but I know of somebody who believes it is much more important than that.' She waited until she had his attention before she said, 'It was Bran who put it into my head.'

Bran was embarrassed. He saw Richard Ramsey turn towards him and he himself got to his feet, prepared to say as little as possible and go. 'I just had the idea,' he said, 'that Mr Harman may have been interested in alchemy.'

Richard Ramsey was startled. 'You know about that, Bernard?'

Bran shook his head. 'No. Only that Harman might be interested.'

Now was the time to go, but Richard Ramsey's hand was on his arm. 'One moment. I have something that may interest you – even if it may disappoint Mr Harman.'

He went to one of the shelves protected by a brass grille. It was locked and he had to return to his desk to fetch a key, but eventually he slid the grille aside and brought down a heavy volume. It had a leather spine without a title, and the pages between the thick boards were rough cut and of uneven sizes.

'This is one exhibit the museum did not have, nor will it.' For so gentle a man there was a steely edge of satisfaction in his voice. 'Potter Waterfall's papers. Collected after his death and bound up willy-nilly by his nearest descendant, an ancestor of mine.'

Sandy knew of it and was uninterested. 'Latin,' she said.

He turned the pages. 'And French. And German. Fortunately only a little Greek.'

'No English,' said Sandy.

'Only a few parts.'

'You never told me.'

'You never wanted to know.'

She got up, and Bran went with her behind the desk. The parchment was brown at the edges and mottled, the penmanship bold but fine, lacking the fussy illegibility of italic, and with only an occasional flourish. A workmanlike hand; a hand that meant business. There were crossings out, notes in the margins, diagrams and sketches over which the writing sometimes wandered and it was at one of these that Richard Ramsey lingered.

'There's a lot about pot-making and glazes,' he

said. He pointed to some sketches of what seemed to be a row of potter's wheels driven by a kind of spit turned by a donkey. Nearby were some formulae. 'Mechanics and chemistry, as you can see.'

Bran uncovered a larger, half-hidden page. 'And the signs of the Zodiac.'

'He was also a philosopher.'

'Alchemist,' said Bran. In spite of the antiquity of the pages, and the sense they gave of secrets revealed, he felt disappointment. A book of spells was a book of boredom; crank's work.

'You are quite right, Bernard. Silas Waterfall sought the Philosopher's Stone.' There was a respect in the way Richard Ramsey spoke that made him suddenly dwindle in Bran's eyes. Any fool could dabble in magic, and only fools had respect for those who did. But then the tone was qualified. 'The old potter was a little out of his time, it's true, but he had all the equipment around him, the furnaces and crucibles, and he knew some chemistry, so I suppose it was natural that a person of his frame of mind should turn that way. He never managed it as far as I know, but it wasn't through want of trying.'

'Managed what?' said Sandy.

Bran quickly glanced at her father but he was turning pages, seeking something, and Bran himself answered. 'He tried to turn base metal into gold.' And then, because he thought she might not have heard the phrase, he added, 'Ordinary metal into gold.'

'Thank you, teacher. I know all about that. I've already been told.'

Her father looked up suddenly. 'Here it is,' he said. 'This is what I wanted to show you, Bernard.'

Sandy butted in. 'All I want to know,' she said, 'is

did they manage it? Did any of them ever turn anything into gold?'

'It's irrelevant.' Her father would have shrugged it away but saw that she was about to insist. 'And who cares? You could turn anything into anything else if you had the equipment. It's only a question of altering structures. They knew it. Those old alchemists knew it, and it became uninteresting. Totally.'

'Not to me,' she said.

'Look at this.' He pointed to the page again. 'This is what I was trying to tell you about Potter Waterfall. He was a philosopher, as they all became, at least the true ones; wanting to purify the human soul much more than wanting to purify metal.'

'Fascinating.' She was full of scorn.

'True, true.' He took the word at its face value. 'Let me read you this.'

He bent his head over the page and began to read:

' "Be it nothing but dross, yet it be put to the true solvent it doth become gold. So with Man, true knowledge shall roll back his darkness as vapours over bright waters." '

'Is it the Bible?' she said. 'I don't get it.'

But her father was seeking a response from Bran. And Bran, suddenly reckless, gave it to him. Potter Waterfall's words had taken him back to the giddy top of the Steps with the plain far below.

'Who wants gold?' he said. 'It's the most worthless thing in the world.'

Richard Ramsey's smile leapt again. 'I need not have worried over you, Bernard. You have the stuff of the true alchemist in you. One of Potter Waterfall's kind.' And he permitted himself a tinge of malice. 'Mr Harman would hardly understand you.'

'And neither do I.' Sandy straightened. 'I think

you're stupid, the pair of you. And nobody has told me yet the most important thing – did he, or did he not, manage to make the stuff? Does that book say?'

Her father shook his head. 'If he did he left it far behind. It became of no importance.'

Sandy grabbed Bran's hand and began to pull him across the room and out of the door. 'Come on,' she said, 'before he says anything even more ridiculous.'

17

Outside the door she stopped.

'Fetch it,' she said.

He knew she meant the box. 'It's safe enough where it is.'

'Fetch it. Or I will.'

She reached for the door handle but he held her wrist and she lurched into him. He waited for the cry of anger that would bring her father out but, in the darkness, her free hand was suddenly behind his neck and her mouth was on his. She squirmed, seeming to flow in and around him, soft and moist, yet urgent. But within an instant she had changed, withdrawing her lips, pushing him away.

'Now will you fetch it?' she said.

It was mercenary, and anger made him turn away. 'It can stay where it is.'

Instantly she was close to him. 'I didn't mean it like that, Brandy. Honestly I didn't.' She was contrite, demure even, but her scented warmth reached him, coaxing him to hold her again. She spoke innocently. 'I just wanted to show you something. Tell him we're going to put it back in its hiding place.'

She was again offering herself. He made a show of resisting, drawing back, but even as he did so he was surrendering. 'All right,' he said.

He turned the handle and went back into the room. Her father merely smiled and handed him the box as he muttered something about wanting to examine it more closely, and after a few seconds he was back in the hall.

'I knew it would be easy for you,' she said. 'He'd only get suspicious with me.' Immediately she began tugging him towards the glass door and the short corridor to the conservatory. It was not until the second door had closed behind them and they were in the shadow of the vine that she faced him.

'Kiss me, Brandy.'

He leant forward to do so but the box was between them and he was clumsy. She giggled and let her lips no more than brush his before she had taken the box from him and walked towards the sundial in the centre of the floor.

'Move it, would you, Bran darling?' She was impersonal now and he tugged at the pedestal savagely, almost hating her for her twists of mood, but he knew he was at her mercy. The sundial was heavier than he thought and he had to struggle before stone grated on stone and the cavity was revealed.

She crouched and put the box on the ground beside her. 'My father doesn't know everything,' she said.

'What is that supposed to mean?' He got down beside her.

'Open the lid.'

Carelessly, still resentful, he obeyed her.

'There,' she said. 'That's what I was going to show you.'

The box was not empty. The dim light from the glass roof showed a dingy shape, like a brown slug, inside it. Gradually he became aware that it was a small flask. 'What's that?' He kept interest out of his voice.

'It's my mother's and it belongs in there.'

'I've not seen it before.'

'Well now you have. Your mother had the box and my mother had that.'

'What is it?'

'Give it to me.'

The box was closer to her than himself and he knew he was being put to some form of test. He lifted the little flask and shook it gently, feeling liquid move inside. 'I still don't know what it is.'

'My father has a theory.' She was watching him closely now. 'Do you notice anything?'

He shook his head. 'What should I notice?'

Gingerly she pressed the flask into his palm. 'Close your fingers,' she said. 'Hold it tight.' He did so. 'Now do you feel anything?'

He concentrated, shaking his head.

'Nothing?'

'Only that my hand's getting sweaty.'

'Yes?'

'Pretty warm.' He opened his fingers quickly. 'Hot even.'

'I knew it.' She was grinning; delighted.

He let the flask roll slightly in his palm. It seemed to make a tiny patch of heat where it touched his skin. He handed it to her and she held it delicately, drawing in her breath.

'I was right,' she said. 'I knew there was something hot inside.'

It was ridiculous. She had half-understood something to which she had barely listened and was jumping to an absurd conclusion. 'It wasn't hot until I touched it,' he said. 'It can't be hot all the time. It got its heat from me.'

'I don't know about that. All I know is that it isn't what my father always says.'

'Which is?'

'That it's just some stupid old glaze for his pots.'

'What is it then, Sandy?'

She detected his aloofness and raised her head suspiciously. 'Never you mind.'

But he persisted. 'It's not the Alcahest, the solvent they used with the Philosopher's Stone to make gold.'

'Who said it was?'

'You're acting as though that's what you think.' She was silent under his scorn and he began to relent. 'It's what your father said it was; old Potter Waterfall's glaze.'

'I don't think Mr Harman would agree.'

He looked at her sharply. She gazed back steadily and for a moment they fenced with each other, she seeking to make him conspire with her in a private fantasy, and he, half reluctantly, resisting her. He was weakening, prepared to be persuaded, but his reaction had not been quite quick enough for her and she suddenly thrust the phial at him. 'Put it back.'

He held it. There was no doubt of the heat now; it must have picked up more from her. He opened his mouth but she would not let him speak.

'Put it back.' She stood up.

He put the flask into the casket and felt it roll to a barely perceptible hollow in the pottery base. The place had been made for it and it was back where it belonged. He closed the lid and lowered the box into the hole in the floor. She watched him, standing back a pace as he began to shift the pedestal. Her mood changed again and she grinned.

'What would little Mr Harman give to know what we know?' she said. 'Even if you sell the box, he won't know that he's missed the most important part.'

'I like to see them together,' he said. 'I don't think I should sell.'

'Please yourself.' She turned abruptly and went back into the house.

18

The dusk had thickened under the trees and Bran was glad of it because Sandy had not forgiven him and the darkness made it easier to keep a distance between them and remain silent as they made their way down the hill towards the village. He was not taken wholly by surprise when she stopped without warning near the lock-keeper's cottage, and he allowed himself to go on a few paces to show that he was not totally obedient to her whims. Suddenly, however, she had gone through the gate and closed it behind her.

'See you later,' she said, and was gone, disappearing in a quick patter of footsteps through the tall hollyhocks and around the end of the cottage.

He kicked at a stone, in a fury with her. She still had him at her mercy. If he waited he would be subservient, and if he returned to the house she would construe it as sulkiness; either way would allow her to look down on him. He kicked again at a stone, listened to it hop away down the path and fall with a faint splash into the canal. The sound drew his eyes to the water and beyond, and a means of escape without ignominy occurred to him. He would go ahead and wait for her in the village.

But he had no sooner moved away from the cottage than doubt crept into his mind. If her friends were there he would not know them; the whole village was still a place of mystery to him. Halfway across the lock gates he caught a glimpse of the stars in the still water below, as though the whole sky had swung down to make a vast hollow beneath him, and he had to cling to the railing against the giddiness. Cautiously he edged towards the far side and stepped down.

It was, for him, stepping into an unknown world. In the alleyway between the buildings it was dark and his footfalls were deadened as though heavy dust had sifted down with the night. The daytime hum of machinery from the pottery had ceased, and ahead of him the square gleamed softly like a lighted room in a deserted house.

He paused on the threshold. The pairs of globes that he had noticed by daylight at either end of the square now glowed like night blooms, distributing a pallid whiteness instead of fragrance, and triple globes that he had not known about hung within the grove and coated the still leaves with a frail luminescence.

In the surrounding houses there were signs of life, a glimpse of lit rooms, and a wedge of yellow light lay on the pavement at the door of the Black Swan, but in the spaces of the square nothing moved. Bran found himself, like a mouse at the wainscot, edging along the side of the square, and only when he had shortened the distance did he cross to the protection of the grove.

But even here, beneath the trees, there was a feeling of formality, the trunks set in a circle almost as regularly spaced as columns, and an ironwork seat at one side matched on the other by an old stone horse trough.

He had been apprehensive about meeting strangers but now the stillness began to unnerve him and he looked beyond the trees hoping for some evidence that he was not entirely alone. He picked out the shop where they had had tea, but the chairs and tables had gone and the blind now shadowed its front like a heavy eyelid drooping into sleep. Nothing anywhere stirred, and suddenly he lost patience with it, stooped, picked up a pebble and threw it towards the trough. He missed, but something, perhaps a night-flying moth, touched the water and made fragments of light dart.

As though his sudden movement had been a signal, two other things happened. He heard laughter and saw Sandy and another girl emerge from the dark alleyway into the square, but, closer at hand, between them and himself, a tall, broad figure grew from the deep shadow of one of the trunks and stood near the trough. The head was facing him, but what little light reached it simplified the features into barred shadows as anonymous as a helmet. Then the laughter came nearer and the helmet head turned in that direction.

It was Sandy, as always, who picked up a glimmer of light in her skin and hair, more so as the girl with her seemed almost invisible, not reflecting or acting against her surroundings but seeming to be absorbed into whatever was shadowy or dark. Yet it was she who first saw that the grove was inhabited and interrupted Sandy's chatter to point towards the standing figure.

'Griff!' Sandy hastened forward. 'Have you seen him?'

Bran heard no reply but something must have been said because her glance travelled into the grove and she spotted him.

'There you are. Why on earth didn't you wait?'

She beckoned him impatiently over, and he moved towards her, but in his own time, letting her see he was not subservient. Other people, attracted by their voices, were joining them in the grove.

'Hurry up! There's nothing to be afraid of. Griff's quite harmless – I think.' She looked at her companion and laughed. The dark girl, her eyes on him, did not smile.

'Stella,' said Sandy, introducing him. She giggled. 'I wonder if you remember each other.'

He bowed slightly, something he had never done towards a person of his own age, yet the occasion and the girl herself seemed to demand it. She had the kind of beauty that went with the night, not the daylight flash and dazzle of Sandy, but something secret that refused to offer itself and had to be sought out. The pale oval of her face was dusted into indefiniteness by the dim light, and her eyes were shadowed with dark lashes that blurred their outline.

'How do you do?' she said, matching his formality, and her voice surprised him. It had a catch in it and undulated between two tones that made it both girlish and womanly. It was disconcerting, alluring and at the same time taunting, and he was still absorbed in all the mysteries she seemed to present, all the retreats in her character that drew his attention after her and away from everything else, when Sandy's voice called him back.

'And this is Griff.' As she spoke, Sandy moved swiftly to Bran's side and clung to his arm, preventing him shaking hands. She spoke to the whole circle. 'Meet Bran,' she said. 'Brandywine, Bran-tub.' She was excited and what she really was saying was Mine, mine, mine. 'But he's very shy and timid. When I went to find you, Stella, he ran away. Didn't you, Bran?'

He tried to avoid the ridicule she seemed to be inviting for him. 'No,' he said. 'I don't run. Never.'

He knew he was too emphatic, but the girl seemed to understand. 'I'm glad of that,' she said.

'There ain't many who don't run at least once.' Griff's voice, for all his size, was a thin wheeze and his little laugh was choked.

The air was thick with misunderstanding and Bran began to speak, trying to re-establish the modesty he seemed to have thrown away, but Sandy did not allow him. 'He's not only brave and handsome,' she said. 'He's rich.'

'Two out of three.' Bran attempted to grin as he eased himself from her grip. 'One of those isn't true.'

Stella saw his embarrassment. 'You're not rich,' she said. 'I can believe the rest.'

'Griff!' cried Sandy, 'are you going to stand for this?' She only increased the awkwardness, and had to continue to speak 'Anyway she's wrong. He *is* rich.'

'And it's the least important thing about him,' said Stella. Bran saw the glimmer of a smile on her mouth but her eyes were too deeply hidden to show any expression.

'But it's the thing I like about him best.' Sandy, losing ground, tried to make a joke of it. 'And he could be even richer. A lot.'

Stella said, 'She seems to know a great deal about you, Bran.' The voice murmured in the quiet grove, defenceless, almost woebegone, but it spurred Sandy into a retort.

'Beware of her, Brandy. She wants to know everything.' Sandy could not completely hide her anger.

'I'm sorry,' said Stella.

'There's no need to be.' Bran defended her.

'Not yet,' said Sandy.

'There's nothing much to tell.' He spoke lightly, trying to reduce the antagonism of the two girls. 'And I'm not going to get rich. You know I'm not, Sandy.'

'You could if you wanted to.' She was almost sulking, and he faced the other girl.

'This is all a bit stupid,' he said. 'It's only a box that somebody wants to buy, but I'm not going to sell. It's not much, really.'

'Oh no.' Sandy was sarcastic.

Stella was turning away, tactfully showing a lack of interest, but Bran could not leave it there. Now that this much had been revealed she was owed some explanation. 'You'll see it soon,' he said, 'because it's going to be on display.' He nodded towards the end of the square and the museum.

'That's the first I've heard of it!' cried Sandy.

He shrugged. He had at that moment seen it as inevitable that the box belonged with the other exhibits. It was not truly his; he wanted no part of it. Sandy had drawn back from him and he awaited another outburst, but Stella's voice came between them.

'Then it is something to do with the picture.'

Sandy whirled. 'How do you know that?'

'I can put two and two together, Sandy.'

'Well you've got the wrong answer.'

'Have I, Bran?' She ignored Sandy.

He looked at Sandy but she shook her head violently, wishing him to say nothing. 'There can't be any harm in telling people,' he said.

'I think there is. But it's up to you.' She turned away.

His eyes were on Stella. He could not go back. 'It's the box,' he said. 'Potter Waterfall's box.'

'And Mr Harman wants to buy it from you.' She spoke as if she was finishing his sentence.

Sandy's head jerked. 'How do you know that? Have you been sneaking about spying?'

'There's been no need to do that.' Stella was unruffled. 'It's no secret that Mr Harman has been staying in the village.'

Sandy was taken aback, but only for an instant. 'Then I do know how you found out.' She advanced on Griff. 'He's the one who's been finding out things he's not supposed to know. Mr Harman has been staying at the Black Swan, and this big lump,' she began to poke him in the chest, 'has been listening at keyholes.'

'Not me.' His strangled little voice sounded almost childish, but his large hand completely enveloped hers and prevented her jabbing at him.

'It must have been. Let go; you're hurting.'

'It's nothing to what I'd do to him if I had him here.' There was real malice in the thin voice and Sandy, making the most of what was presented to her, remained close to him.

'What did he do to you, Griff? Didn't you get a big enough tip?'

'I threw his bloody money in the canal!'

'Why was that, Griff? Did he bully you?'

'Nobody bullies me! Nobody!' Yet he felt the grip of the humiliating handshake and his own fingers tightened on hers.

'I believe you!' she cried. 'Get him off, somebody, he's hurting!'

He released her.

'You don't know your own strength.' She made no attempt to back away from him. 'Why is it you dislike him so much?' She had softened her voice, coaxing him.

'I just do, that's all.'

'I thought he was a nice little man. Lovely sharp white teeth. I don't want you hurting him, you great bully.' All of her antagonism towards Stella seemed to have been forgotten. Now she was flattering Griff, blatantly, and he preened.

'He just better keep on my right side next time, that's all,' he said.

'What if he doesn't?' She began to taunt him.

'I'll chuck *him* in the canal.'

'Next time he does what?'

But Griff saw the trap and shrugged.

'You wouldn't dare,' she said.

'Wouldn't I?'

'You wouldn't dare do that to anybody.'

And then she shrieked because in one swift movement he had scooped her off her feet and spun round with her.

'Stop it, Griff! Put me down!' But as she yelled she was laughing, clinging to his neck.

'Do you still say I daren't?' He walked with her to the trough and held her above the water.

'Let me go!'

He began to lower her and her tone became more urgent.

'My dress is in the water! I'm getting wet, you big idiot!'

'Say you're sorry.'

'No.'

'Say it.'

'No!' She was angry now, struggling and battering at his shoulder. 'You great coward! Let me go!'

His only answer was to stoop further forward, and whatever humour and teasing there had been between them vanished. She was twisting desperately to keep clear of the water, almost whimpering.

'I would stop now, if I were you,' said Bran.

The stooping back stiffened. Sandy lay still. There

was a moment's doubt as to what would happen and then Griff made as if to lower her still further.

'Don't do it,' said Bran.

The broad shoulders came up and Griff turned, still holding her. Then he let her legs swing to the ground and his voice came scratching at Bran from the helmet head. 'You say something?'

Bran knew that all he had to do was change his tone, make light of it. He had no animosity towards the big man. But suddenly any choice was taken from him.

Sandy raised her voice. 'He told you to let me go!'

Griff's arm remained around her waist.

'Let me go!' As she shouted she slapped him across the face. It was a hard blow and the crack of it brought silence.

Griff said nothing and did not even appear to move but his arm tightened, unbearably, and she cried out in real pain.

Her cry set Bran moving. Afterwards he remembered Stella putting out a hand to hold him back, and there was a scratch on his arm where he had shaken her off, but at the time he did not feel it.

19

Sandy was pushed roughly to one side before Bran was halfway towards them. She staggered slightly before she regained her balance and nervously pushed back the hair that had fallen across her brow. She had been frightened.

'Do you always treat girls like that?' Bran's voice was level, surprising himself. His heart thudded.

'Like what?' The words issued reedily from a face in the shadow.

'Like a coward.'

It was a ritual. The watchers, seeming to fill all the spaces between the trunks around them, were silent. Suddenly Bran wanted to yell at them, break free of the ridiculous performance that was beginning, start again, but they ringed him like a palisade, quite motionless, waiting.

Bran had stopped near Sandy. Now Griff's heavy figure was in motion, coming towards him, drifting easily and without sound over the dusty earth. He stopped two paces distant.

'What was that you said?' In the broad face the small monkey eyes darted with a dangerous, sneaking malevolence.

'Coward,' said Bran.

The back of Griff's hand, unseen, from nowhere, caught him high on the cheekbone. His head jerked and, with the pain, rage came. Yet he kept his hands at his sides. Kept them there for the one tiny advantage he had over the fighter.

'Now say it again.' Griff had stepped back and was poised, fists waist-high.

Bran stood very still.

'Once more, pretty boy,' the voice squeaked. 'And then I'll kill you.'

Bran did not move.

'Jesus!' In disgust, Griff straightened from his crouch. 'Pretty boy's had enough already.'

Bran moved with a swiftness that was elegant. Shoulder, arm, fist were in line and the thick lips burst like paper under his knuckles. The solid figure went back, staggered, almost fell, then Griff was bending forward with his hands on his knees as his blood dotted the dust at his feet.

Bran waited. He had used up his one advantage: catching Griff off-guard. He had either succeeded or he would have to pay. Almost idly he lifted his eyes to the watchers among the trees. They murmured but did not move, and he, like them, brought his eyes back to the arena.

Slowly, Griff wiped the blood from his mouth along his arm and stood up. He took his time and then came in professionally, head sheltered behind fists and shoulder. Bran parried the first punch on his forearm as he was meant to do. The second came through the gap and into his ribs.

Both girls heard the thud of the fist and saw the blond head dip and jerk like a stem lashed by a gale. His whole body sank and his mouth opened, gasping against the piercing pain in his chest. The next blow finished the fight.

Bran twisted and saw the busy fists and shoulders

above him picking their point; and the executioner's face concentrating.

He uncurled, swinging up into the heart of destruction at the instant he expected to be felled. His fist jarred once more against bone. It made a crack like the sound of a whip, clean and final.

Then he was upright, not even panting, and the dark figure was sliding down in front of him, dwindling and collapsing.

'Hell!' One of the watchers among the trees let his breath out on the syllable.

Bran stood where he was and slowly Sandy came up to him. She said nothing but she touched his arm and then let her hand fall until her fingertips slid over his slippery knuckles.

The dark girl was crouching over the darker figure. The indistinct shape changed as she heaved at him, raising Griff's head, levering him to one elbow.

'Is he all right?' said Bran.

She lifted her face and it caught a glimmer of light from between the leaves. There was no depth in her eyes, nor softness, only a cold shallowness.

Sandy tugged at his arm. 'Come on,' she said. 'Let's go.'

20

'Bran!' Sandy's whisper came through the door just as he had taken off his shirt.

'Bran!' She was tapping quietly but urgently.

He dropped his shirt by the wash-basin and crossed the room. Caution made him switch off the light before he reached for the handle, but she must have been holding it on the other side because the instant he touched it the door opened and she pushed by him in the darkness. A faint smell of apples from the landing swirled around them as she closed the door softly and leant against it. She sighed with relief.

'What's the matter?' he said.

'Sh!' She hushed him. 'They'd go mad if they knew I was here.'

'Has anything happened?' he whispered.

'I was worried about you, that's all. I came to see how you were.'

Her sympathy was belated. All the way up the hill she had chattered about anything but the fight, almost as though it had never taken place. And she had sent him to his room swiftly and secretly, keeping him out of the way of her parents.

'I'm all right,' he said.

'But all that blood!'

'Mostly his. I was just going to wash it off.'

In the darkness she raised his hand and put his knuckles against her cheek.

'I wouldn't do that,' he said. 'Too much blood and dust.'

She trembled. 'I'm ever so sorry it had to happen, Bran. It was all because of me.'

'I don't think so.'

'Oh yes it was. I've been thinking. That's why I had to come to see you.' She paused. 'Bran?'

'Yes.'

'I was jealous. I thought you were going to tell her everything; everything about what's in the box. I didn't want you to, Bran. I wanted us to have a secret.'

'I'm sorry.'

'That's why I was nasty.' She was close to him, whispering, but in the darkness almost invisible. 'I couldn't sleep till I'd told you.'

He reached for her but she backed away, still holding his hand.

'I saw you look at her, Bran.'

He gave a little despairing laugh. 'Well I had to do that to talk to her.'

'You thought she was pretty, I could see that. I was jealous.'

'I don't even remember what she looked like.'

'That's not true.'

She fell silent and seemed to shrink from him. An enormous pity for her swept over him and he heard himself say, 'It's you I remember.'

There was silence for a moment, and then she spoke very softly. 'Oh, Bran.'

Contempt for himself made his voice croak slightly as he said, 'I mean it.'

He expected her to come towards him but once again she retreated, moving further across the room. But she tugged him with her.

'Anyway she doesn't know everything.' Her voice was happy, all doubts gone. 'You didn't tell her about what's inside the box. And wouldn't she like to know?'

She had changed her dress for something longer and of a flimsier material so that although she moved quickly, leading him across the room, there was no sound of it rustling, merely the sense of it floating out and spreading her warmth.

She held his hands in the basin and ran cold water over them.

'What are you wearing?' he asked.

'I'm ready for bed.' She laughed, almost feverishly. 'But don't you get any ideas; I'm quite decent.' She held out a towel and smothered his hands. 'There's one thing I haven't said yet, Bran.'

'What's that?'

'Thank you for rescuing me from that great brute. He nearly dropped me in the water, he really did.'

He remembered her squealing in Griff's arms and said, 'I thought you were enjoying it.'

'Now you're being nasty to me.' Her head drooped and he knew she was pouting. 'All I was saying was how brave you were. Nobody else would have dared.'

He grasped her hands through the towel and drew her closer. Her face tilted up to show him wide open eyes and parted lips. She shrank nearer but still their lips did not touch.

'I'd better go,' she whispered. 'I don't dare.'

His hands still held hers. 'Stay for a while. I won't harm you.'

He led her to where the open window gaped into the huge night beyond the hill. He wanted to sit on the wide window-ledge with her but she refused.

'Somebody might see.'

'There's nobody there.'

'Foxes,' she said, and giggled.

She drew him back into the room and sank to the floor. 'I'll sit here if you like.'

He lowered himself beside her. They were half on and half off the carpet. The polished boards were cool and uneven under his hand.

Suddenly she let herself be kissed, leaning towards him, her head back. 'Brandy,' she said, and her hair brushed his bare shoulder. They sank down until her head rested on his arm on the floor. He held his face above hers. 'You smell of apples,' he said.

In the grainy light her eyes had an uncertain edge, patches of indistinct darkness in which anything could be happening. He touched her lips again. They were soft and damp.

'Apples?' she said. 'Is that nice?'

'Or plums.' He slid his legs back so that he lay face down on the carpeted boards beside her, 'You are more like a plum.'

'Plum?' She put her hands on either side of his face and held him inches from her. 'Why plum?'

The word suited her lips and he was giddy with need for her.

'A plum is very soft,' he said. 'Like this.' He touched her mouth and at the same time put one arm across her body. But as he did so her fingers pressed on the bruise Griff had made high on his temple. She saw him wince.

'You're a wounded soldier,' she said.

'It doesn't matter. I hardly feel it.'

'You were wounded when you rescued me.'

'I'd do it again.'

She opened her mouth. 'This is a reward for a soldier.' She kissed him.

'Give the soldier a plum.'

134

She kissed him again. 'There now.'

He held his mouth on hers. 'He wants another one.'

'There isn't another one.'

'Oh yes there is.' He moved the arm that lay across her, expecting her to push it aside, but all she did was to slide her hands from his face to his shoulders. She tried to dig her fingers into his muscles.

'You are like iron, Brandy. You are too strong.'

'I'm gentle.'

'You're dangerous.'

'But it's me who is afraid of you,' he said.

Their breath mingled.

'You needn't be,' she said.

'May the soldier advance?'

'It all depends where he's going.'

'Just a long a smooth highway.' He moved his hand.

'What does he want?'

'A plum.'

'What if the cupboard's locked?'

'He'll try persuasion.'

He lowered his face to hers and very softly brushed her lips. Her head rolled back along his arm and she relaxed utterly, suddenly fell apart like the petals of a dying flower spread on the same hard boards that pressed against his belly and thighs.

She was so flimsy he was barely aware he was touching her; so moist she fell away as he approached. Very slowly she brought her face back to him.

'The cupboard opened,' she murmured. 'Has he found what he wanted?'

'You know he has.'

Their lips were fierce now and suddenly she arched herself, her nails digging into his shoulder. The boards ground into him.

'Soldier!'

The night reached in through the window, cool, like steel, and held them. They struggled to match its grip. Tightening. Tightening. Till it sang and broke.

Then they lay where they were, ceasing to think, letting the air as it flooded down from the hill cool them.

The expanding night suddenly contracted. From outside, at the foot of the house, there came a faint sliding sound. A door was being closed softly. They raised their heads, listening.

'I told you!' Alarm made her panic. 'There's somebody out there!'

Bran crawled swiftly to the window and looked over the sill. Under the stars the hillside tumbled down to the house in a mass of black shadows which stopped only at the edge of the glass of the conservatory which lay as still as grey water below him. It was impossible to penetrate its metallic surface, but that was where the sound had come from, the only door it could have been was there. He strained his eyes, but the leaves made many hiding places and he saw nothing.

He crept back to where Sandy was now sitting, stiffly upright. She seemed too afraid to move.

'Could it be your father?'

She shook her head. 'He's in bed long ago. They both are.'

Bran went to the door and listened. The house was quiet. He opened the door and looked out. No light glimmered anywhere.

He went back to her, found his shirt and put it on. 'Come on.'

This time he led the way, holding her hand. They were barefoot, and the thick carpet on the stairs helped them to move silently. They were no more than gliding shadows as they went down into the corridor leading to the conservatory. At the second door he peered through the glass panels. Nothing stirred.

Slowly he turned the handle and pushed the door open. The room was utterly still. He stepped inside, drawing her with him. The motionless plants around them were vaguely threatening, as though the presence of strangers had forced them to arrest some secret movement in their growing.

She was touching his back, afraid to let him move out of reach as she followed him across the stone floor to the outer door. He tried it. It swung open. He felt a tingle along his muscles, and Sandy gasped.

'There was somebody!' she whispered. 'There must have been!'

They thought of the same thing together and turned abruptly and went back to the sundial.

'Let's see,' he said.

He bent over, putting his arms around it, ready to pull it aside. But, on the verge of moving, he held himself rigid.

'Bran!' she said. 'What's wrong?'

'Nothing. Just getting a better grip.' He took the weight this time and moved the pedestal.

Before it had come to rest, she was down on her knees lifting the box from the cavity.

'Thank God!' she sat back. 'It's there. All of it.'

He went to lock the door. 'I should think it was a breeze,' he said as he came back. 'Or one of your foxes.'

She was prepared to believe him. 'Guilty conscience,' she said.

He smiled. 'Put it back and we'll go.'

He watched her lower the box into the hole. There was something he ought to tell her. Yet he held back.

'Careful does it,' he said, and began to move the pedestal. He aligned its base with the crevices between the flagstones of the floor. This was what he had not told her. He had left the pedestal standing square on the flagstones, as her father also would have done if he had been the last one to move it – not at an angle over the lines; not as he had found it a moment ago.

He slid the pedestal and listened to the grating sound it made. Now he was sure; doubly sure. Just before the closing of the door had alarmed them, this was the sound he had heard. Somebody, so recently he almost felt the warmth of their hands on the stone, had been examining their hiding place.

2 1

Bran woke early. Only the faintest grey light reached the window and it hardly penetrated the darkness of the room. He was bedded deep within the cells of the house and it slept around him without a sound, not even the faint murmuring of deep night. He stirred, vaguely dissatisfied, and then, quite suddenly, he had slid from the warm sheets and was getting dressed.

The clothes from the fight were in a bundle under the wash-basin, and he found a dark shirt and faded jeans in the depths of the wardrobe. He caught a glimpse of himself in the long mirror as he buckled the broad belt, his fair hair almost white in the between-light and flattened by sleep to the sides of his head. He was like a ghost in the room, and he swung the door to shut the image away.

Barefoot, carrying his sandals, he went out into the warmth of the landing. The heart of the house was absolutely silent, as though inviting him to curl on the carpet and sleep, but he drifted downwards and through the hall to the glass doors of the conservatory. They clicked to behind him and he walked across the cool stone to the sundial. He stopped, half intending to inspect the contents of the cavity, but the base did not appear to have been moved since he left it, and when he tried the outer door it was still locked. He slid his toes into the straps of his sandals and went out.

In the dimness the garden was grey and the stillness

was deepened by the tick of dew dropping from stooping, colourless flowers. He mounted the slope to the edge of the forest before he looked down at the house. It was no more than a dark patch among the trees like some animal crouched under damp fur, still huddled in its night resting place. He was free of it. He turned his back and let the soles of his sandals slap his feet as he walked into the trees.

He flushed a few birds from fern patches, but most were in the treetops and as he climbed he heard them begin to greet the day high overhead. He began to run, wanting to clear the dimness of the trees before the sun showed, and his ears were full of the sound of his own breath and the pounding of his feet when, quicker than he expected, he emerged.

He stopped. Ahead of him the rock slab ran out into space, making its own horizon halfway up the pale sky. A low mist clung to it like wisps of the receding night. No birds dared sing here.

He went forward silently on the moss and stood at the edge of the first pool. The water, held so far above the earth, was untarnished. Water plants showed through it without blemish, bright green and pure.

He raised his eyes. Potter Waterfall's Steps shelved away in green platforms that ended jaggedly above dunes of white cloud that had piled up in the long tide of the night and now stretched as far as he could see in motionless ridges. Almost, at this giddy height, he could feel the earth tilting downwards towards the sun. He watched the paleness in the distance burn as the earth dipped in its long curve and on its back pulled him after Africa down the sky, and he went with it, leaping from step to step, as the clouds were raked by the sun's first rays.

He came down to the level where the hut was built,

and the platforms below it disappeared into the solidifying pearly greyness so that the cloud floor stretched away almost from his feet. He was careless and easy now and splashed through the pools, but even this disturbed nothing, for the sound was deadened almost before it began and the vegetation beneath the water rose to obliterate his footsteps. He was watching it happen and did not raise his head until he was a few paces from the hut.

She was huddled on the steps, a dark blanket around her shoulders, and she was watching him as unblinking as a cat.

'I thought I was alone,' he said feebly. Even in daylight there was a hidden quality in Stella's looks, a carelessness, as though she herself distrusted beauty and would deny it. Yet it was hers. And in unexpected ways. Her eyes startled him. He had assumed that, like her hair, they were black, yet now he could see that beyond their dark fringes they were blue; a deep blue that was turned towards him, telling him nothing.

'I'm sorry about last night,' he said, and when no flicker of understanding crossed her face, he added, 'The fight.'

Still nothing from her.

'I hope he's not hurt.'

She spoke then, briefly. 'Of course he was hurt.'

'Not badly, I mean. I didn't want to hurt him badly.'

'You hit him.'

'It was a lucky punch. He could take me apart at any time.'

'If you let him.'

He shrugged. 'I may have no choice.'

'That's one thing you always have,' she said. 'You can fight; you can run away.' She removed her eyes from him and looked beyond the Steps into space.

'I shall not fight him again,' he said. She made no reply and he looked beyond her to the open door at the back of the verandah. Inside the hut a canvas day bed had been pulled to the centre of the floor, and a crumpled blanket similar to the one around her shoulders lay on it.

'You've been here all night,' he said.

'I sleep here from time to time,' she said. 'When I feel like it.'

'I didn't know.'

'I have permission.'

'I didn't mean that,' he said.

'Then what did you mean?' The blanket cut a diagonal across her face making her cheek as round as a child's, and her voice had the catch in it that made her appear so vulnerable.

'I mean that you can do just what you like.'

'Thank you, sir.' The sarcasm was ruined by the fact that she felt her eyes suddenly brim with tears. He seemed so lonely and so lost, standing there in front of her, as though he did not belong.

'I don't own this place,' he said. 'I'm a stranger here.'

'Then why don't you go away? You've brought nothing but trouble.' She heard herself being cruel, needlessly, punishing herself as she punished him, but it was unbearable to see him stand there, so forlorn, like a small boy.

'When I get a chance,' he said, 'I'll go.'

She turned away then, and he saw the edge of the blanket furtively raised to her eyes.

'Stella,' he said.

She half turned towards him, letting him see her profile.

'You weren't like this last night,' he said.

She shook her head, unable to speak.

'What's changed, then? I've told you I'm sorry about Griff.'

'I don't care about Griff.' It was true; she didn't. 'He can have that . . . that horrible cousin of yours for all I care.'

'They were just playing about, Stella. It didn't mean anything.'

'Then after that she plays about with you. That's just what she likes. She hasn't changed a bit – ever!'

And suddenly he remembered that this was the girl who, according to Sandy, had refused to go into the hut all of those years ago; the little girl he had almost forgotten ever existed.

'So you can go back to her,' she said. 'You and Griff both. She's welcome. How long do you think it'll be before she's letting him into the secrets as she did you last night?'

For a moment his mind reeled. How could Stella know what had happened in his room? But there had been the noise that startled them; that had made him leap to the window. But that was downstairs; the conservatory . . . and then he knew.

'So it was you,' he said.

She was standing now, still wearing the blue dress of the night before, with the blanket bundled in her arms.

'You,' he repeated.

'Meaning?'

'The sundial. Last night.' He watched. The flicker of apprehension in her was unmistakable. 'You moved it.'

She knew she had given too much away. 'What if I did? I took nothing.' It was a guttersnipe's defence and he brushed it aside.

'How did you know?'

'You don't think she can keep anything to herself long, do you?'

'She told you nothing of that.' He was quite certain.

'Maybe not. But she showed me the hiding place years ago.'

'So you kept watch?'

'I did. And I saw you two go there together. And heard what you said.'

'But why?'

She had dropped her eyes and he thought that shame had silenced her. But it was something else. She did not know why she had done it; all that she knew was that it had been vital to find out, as though she had been forced to do it. In the turmoil of her mind she sought for a reason, something to explain it to herself as well as to him. She breathed deeply and raised her head.

'I did it because I had a right to do it!'

She waited to be challenged but he said nothing.

'Your cousin boasts of what *she* has, what *she* owns, what *she* can do that I can't! She makes a great show of being friendly but she keeps me out of things. Suddenly she has a secret.' Stella paused and encouraged the contempt to pour into her voice. 'A precious little secret that nobody else must know. Something so special that all she can do is hint and giggle. Well now she hasn't got a secret, because I know!'

He opened his mouth but she would not let him speak.

'You're the same. There's a pair of you. You thought you'd keep me out of the secret of what's in that stupid, idiotic little box. Well you didn't!'

She turned her back on him. She was panting,

terrified that he would question her motives, for she knew now where the truth lay, yellow-eyed as a snake, lurking in the back of her mind. Her jealousy was a cloak; she had a task she had been paid for and she was afraid to disobey. She *had* to let Harman know what was being hidden from him.

She looked over her shoulder at him. 'So you can go away and tell what you've found out.'

He opened his mouth to reply but she stepped inside the hut and shut the door.

22

The light was still dim in the hall and the house was silent. He could get back to his room before anybody was up and he need not talk about where he had been. He wanted to keep the encounter with the angry, contemptuous girl to himself.

Bran closed the door quietly behind him, slid his feet from his sandals and stooped to pick them up.

'Good morning, Bernard.'

The skin at the back of his neck prickled. He could not even make out where the voice came from. Slowly, as he uncurled from his guilty crouch, he became aware of the outline of Richard Ramsey at the far end of the dark corridor under the stairs. Not trusting his voice, he nodded. As though it had been a signal the man disappeared into the kitchen and he followed.

The tall figure, moving between the dresser and the table, was efficiently setting places for breakfast. 'I have made some tea. I generally have a cup before I take one up to Martha.'

It was an invitation, and Bran advanced, the edges of his jeans, wet with dew, scraping the stone floor. He owed an explanation. 'I woke early and couldn't sleep,' he said. 'I went for a walk.' He did not say in which direction.

'I know. I saw you go.' Richard Ramsey fetched a cup and put it at the end of the table alongside his own. He smiled. 'I'm sorry if I alarm you, Bernard. I had no wish to spy. I'm always up at this time.'

He pulled out a chair for Bran and they sat facing each other across the table. The tea was scalding but when it touched his lips Bran realized how thirsty he was. The man sensed his enjoyment and raised the teapot ready to pour again. There were no questions.

At length Bran said, covering up the subject he did not want to talk about, 'I didn't know potters had to start this early.'

'There's clay to knock up, Bernard. Dirty corners to clean out. A mountain of paper work.'

Richard Ramsey was wearing his usual clay-stained shirt and, like Bran himself, faded jeans. They were the clothes of a labourer, not those of somebody about to face a day's desk work.

'You don't do all that, do you?' Bran asked and the keen eyes looked at him quizzically, not understanding. 'The sweeping up. You don't do that.'

'But why not?'

'Because you're the boss.' He reddened, but kept his gaze steady.

The long, rather grey face was troubled. 'Is that how you see me?'

'No.' Bran defended himself. 'Of course not.'

'Then I'm glad. I do not wish to be anybody's master.'

'I can see that.' Bran's impatience showed and he did not care. 'But it's what you are. You own the place and you can't avoid it. You *are* the master.'

He had raised his voice, speaking like a schoolmaster to a pupil. Now he waited for the consequences.

For a moment Richard Ramsey was silent and then he said, 'You force uncomfortable truths upon me, Bernard. You are the Devil's advocate.'

'I'm sorry.'

He was smiling. 'No, my dear chap. The Devil's advocate is the angel with the fiery burning sword. Be him. You are quite right. That is what I am – the boss.'

The word did not sound proper on his lips and Bran was tempted to relent – but the image of the dark girl who only a short while ago had stood over him thrust itself into his mind. Her words had bitten into his weaknesses; why should Richard Ramsey avoid the same scouring?

'If you are the boss,' he said, 'you have to behave like the boss.'

'Dominate?' The eyebrows were raised and the eyes were innocent. He really wanted to know. 'Do you mean I *should* dominate?'

'Don't you?' Devil's advocacy was heady. Bran felt limitless power to dissect the man in front of him. 'For all the fact that you get up early to sweep the floors for your people, you dominate them.'

'From underneath?' Humour gleamed for a moment and was extinguished. 'I've never sacked anybody.'

'You don't have to sack anybody to dominate. Those who dominate most completely need never sack anybody, because everybody does their will. As they do yours.'

'I do not domineer, Bernard.'

'Of course not. You have the cunning of persuasion.'

'Worse than domineering?'

Bran shrugged. 'More subtle.' He was so much in command he could not leave it there. 'More dangerous. You can see a man clearly when he domineers but when he is a persuader you are never sure where he is.'

'He is kinder,' said Richard Ramsey.

'But is he as honest?'

They drank their tea, regarding each other over the rims of their cups, neither prepared to argue further. Impasse.

At length Richard Ramsey, rubbing the palms of his hands on his knees, consciously changed the subject. 'I'm glad somebody else watches the sunrise from Potter Waterfall's Steps.'

Bran was not sure what he meant. Was he talking about Bran himself, or did he mean Stella? He could tell nothing from the profile presented to him and chose to cover up once more.

'I don't imagine he was like you,' he said. 'Potter Waterfall. He would not do all the drudgery. I can't imagine that.' The portrait was in his mind, the old man in robes seated in a chair like a throne. It was impossible to think of him sweeping floors.

'You are very much mistaken, Bernard.' The eyes were bright, full of something so close to hero-worship that Bran's antagonism stirred again. 'You forget he was a scientist. He knew medicine so he visited the sick, he knew mechanics so he devised his own machinery, and apart from all that he was an artist and an architect. It wasn't only the pots, you know, Bernard, it was the whole village. He made it.'

'And ruled it.' Bran sought out the dark side. No one man could have so many perfections. 'It was he who decided what everybody should do in his village.'

'Maybe. Perhaps. But he also fetched wood for the furnaces and shovelled ashes. He was a complete man.'

'Oh, much more than that.' Bran's impatience returned. 'Don't forget the alchemy.'

Richard Ramsey saw at last that he was being mocked, and a kind of dullness came over his face and his eyes fell.

'There must be something very special in that

flask.' Bran felt a relentless urge to destroy the man's innocence. 'And something just as special in the box. Suppose it has the Philosopher's Stone in the base. Suppose that's what Harman wants to get. And suppose he's right, and that's what it is.'

'That is ridiculous, Bernard.'

'No it's not. It makes sense.' Bran felt his throat tighten until the pain was almost unendurable but he had to say it. 'It makes sense of the bad luck that my mother believed in. It makes sense of what happened.' He glared at his uncle, forbidding him to contradict. 'That's the only thing that makes sense.'

There was anguish in the long, thin face. His uncle said only one word – 'Bernard' – and then fell silent.

They faced each other for long seconds and then Bran forced himself to speak. 'But don't worry. He's never going to get the chance to bargain over it with me, or anybody ever again.'

'You will destroy it?'

Bran shook his head. 'I shall let Potter Waterfall have it back. It can stay with all the rest under his picture in your museum.'

The clouds vanished from Richard Ramsey's face and he reached out to shake Bran's hand.

'Bernard,' he said, 'will you forgive a flight of fancy?'

Bran nodded.

'The old Potter was not mistaken. The box has brought out true gold this morning.' He released Bran's hand and picked up the tray. He was still chuckling to himself as he left the kitchen.

23

Sandy knew nothing. She was late down for breakfast and found Bran in the garden, reading.

'Mother says I've got to take you down and show you the pottery. Father's expecting us.' She grimaced. 'It's your own fault.'

She tried to knock the book from his hand and a moment later they were struggling over it on the grass. He had his arm around her.

'Stop it,' she said. 'Someone will see.'

'You always say that.'

'I mean it!'

She pushed him away and they sat on the lawn with a yard of grass between them.

'At least it'll get your head out of that stupid book,' she said.

She knew nothing. Nobody had told her that he had been out at dawn, and it had not yet filtered through from her father that the museum was to have the box. If she had known anything she could not have prevented herself saying so.

They went down the hill together. She wore a short embroidered jacket and cotton trousers – 'We shall have to climb ladders so I've got to be careful.'

'What do you mean?'

'Skirts.' She laughed. 'Not everybody's got your privileges, randy Brandy.' And she ran ahead of him.

He caught up with her by the lock-keeper's cottage.

'What do you think?' she said, turning her head to look at the little house crouched among its flowers, 'Shall we go and make the peace?' She touched the bruise on his temple and laughed when he winced. 'She can see the wound her man made. It might make her feel better.'

She opened the gate and he followed her along the path. She did not even pause at the front door, saying, 'There's no point in knocking; everybody goes round the back.'

Hollyhocks and marigolds bordered the path, and honeysuckle climbed the side of the house, giving out a heavy scent in which bees murmured with a hum like electricity. At the back there was a paved patch alongside a little outhouse from which, through its open window and door, there came faint sounds of activity.

Sandy crept forward, pulling him with her. Stella, with her back to the window, was ironing, but with a book propped open on a shelf in front of her. Sandy put her fingers to her lips, suppressing a giggle, as the other girl's elbow moved slower and slower and eventually stopped so that she stood, with the iron tilted back on its heel, and all her attention was on the page she was reading. Sandy, anticipating some big indiscretion, was prepared to laugh aloud the moment it came, and Bran could see just beyond the curve of the reading girl's cheek that her mouth was open, childlike, totally absorbed. She was utterly defenceless and he could not allow her to be betrayed. Deliberately, he let his foot scrape the ground.

For a moment it seemed that Stella had heard nothing but then she turned slowly and at the same time began to lift above her head the housewifely flowered apron she wore. She spoke while she was still shaking her hair free of the apron strap, not looking at them. 'I was just going to make myself a cup of coffee,' she said. 'You can go in.'

It was anti-climax for Sandy and she did not disguise it but made straight for the back door. Bran paused just long enough to see Stella turn her book face down on the shelf before she followed. Like almost everything she did, it was closing a door on her privacy.

'I love this.' Sandy crossed the tiny, crowded room and sat on the black horsehair sofa that occupied almost the whole of one wall. She wriggled on it and gave a little shriek. 'It prickles your legs even through your trousers.' She squirmed again. 'Come and try it, Brandy.'

'I wouldn't,' said the girl behind him. 'It's very uncomfortable.' She was on the defensive, ashamed of her surroundings.

Bran said, 'It's just like home.'

The blue eyes focused on him sharply, giving away more in a single glance than he had seen before. She was seeing him as a condescending stranger from the house on the hill, putting an enormous gulf between them when he had intended the opposite.

'Home.' He emphasized the word. 'Where I was brought up. It was like this.'

All three understood what was happening and he pulled out a chair and sat at the table, looking around for something to talk about to relieve the tension. The room was, in a sense, more primitive than his parents' house, but more comfortable, enclosing them. It was, to him, country as against town, even to the thick green cloth that covered the table and was soft and slippery under his palm. The whole room seemed to exist in the shelter of the high black fireplace with the jutting mantle, and at first he was uncertain whether they were in a living room or kitchen. There were old pictures, prints mainly, in heavy frames, and these made it a living room, yet in the corner near the door there was a low cupboard, more like a kitchen cabinet, on which Stella was now placing an electric kettle. Its lead came through a duct near the ceiling and, as she disappeared again through the door, he guessed that the switch was in the outhouse.

Sandy leaned across the table. 'Say something about last night,' she breathed. 'Be nice to her.'

'I already have.'

'When?'

'This morning. At the top of the hill.' He told her about it, and watched her face harden.

'You said nothing.' She was frowning.

He was about to explain, saying he had not had a chance to tell her, and knowing it was an untruth, when he was saved by Stella's reappearance.

'Do you both take sugar?' she asked.

Sandy, sitting upright on the sofa in the manner of an offended matron, spoke tartly. 'I'm surprised you find it necessary to ask,' she said.

In the act of putting cups on a tray, Stella paused. 'Why do you say that?' The catch in her voice gave her an air of absolute innocence.

'You know very well. Something you chose to keep hidden from me. Both of you.'

The clear outline of Stella's lips and eyes against the paleness of her skin made Bran almost gasp. It was a purity that should never be allowed to change.

'She did not know we had already met this morning,' he said to her. 'It's my fault, Stella.'

Understanding dawned. 'Mine too,' she said.

They did not take their eyes from each other, even

allowing Sandy to get to her feet before they turned to her.

'I'm sorry,' he said.

She ignored him.

'We both are.'

'Both!' Sandy put loathing into the word. He waited, because he knew there was more to come. 'I always knew she was sly, but I didn't expect it of you. Not until this moment.' Sandy's face was brightly hard. 'But I see now what you're like – or what she's made of you. You're the same now, the pair of you.'

She pushed by them and was gone. The sound of her steps diminished outside the house, and for as long as she could be heard they kept their heads bowed as though they were concentrating on some dim, retreating music. Then he raised his head.

'I'd better catch up with her,' he said. She nodded and he hesitated before he went on. 'It doesn't matter what she said about you – about us. She lost her temper. Her words don't mean anything.'

She tilted her head so that her hair hid her face. She said nothing.

'Anyway' – he tried to make light of it – 'we're the same, you and me, she said so.'

She lifted her face. Her eyes were blurred and tears were wet on her cheeks. 'Go away.'

It was merely one more pain she would suffer in silence.

'No. I stay.'

He moved around the table towards her. She did not make any attempt to keep him at a distance. Her eyes seemed to accuse him as though it was he, and not Sandy, who was at fault, but he stopped and his lips touched hers. It was he who was sly and deceitful now, without any doubt.

As he tasted the salt of her tears she gave a convulsive little movement and her hands gripped him by the elbows, briefly. Then she was pushing him away.

'Don't,' she said. 'Don't do that again.'

'I want to. It's you I want.'

She shook her head and pushed him further away.

'It's you,' he said. 'I knew it this morning.' He waited and she let her eyes rest on his. 'You knew too.'

She shook her head. 'Follow her,' she said.

'No.'

'You've got to.'

'It's no good. I'll only come back.'

'You're sorry for me. It'll be different later.'

'No!'

'You don't know me yet. She speaks the truth. I am sly. You can't trust me.'

'I don't care!' He moved towards her but again she pushed him back.

'Leave me alone.' She had made up her mind and gradually he retreated. She followed, hesitantly, always at three steps distance, until he was outside in the sun and she was in the doorway. He began to speak again but she dipped her head, refusing to listen, and very slowly, as though to hide herself from him, she went back into the shadow of the room and closed the door.

24

Sandy kept out of his way and Bran did not seek her out. At meal times she ate hastily, said very little and soon departed, and he made excuses to her parents and kept to his room.

The afternoon and then the evening wore away and it was dusk, almost night, before he let himself out of the house and went down the hill. No matter what lay in store for him, he had to see Stella.

He slowed as he neared her cottage and lingered in the shadows that had piled up beneath the trees, but nothing stirred and the blank windows gazed at him as though defying him to seek her out. Perhaps she was not even there. He retreated, turning off the path before he reached the lock gates until he reached the old towpath and wandered along it, through the rank weeds, with the canal between him and the village.

Ahead of him, where the houses ended, he glimpsed the jetty. From there he would be able to see across the canal to the steps leading up into the village; he may be able to see who was in the square.

The trees had begun to encroach, but the jetty still had a broad landing stage on which a cool light played from across the water where the two pale globes marked the steps. He came out into the open.

The square was empty, the water was motionless beneath him, and on the jetty itself the spaced uprights of the bollards where once barges had tied up threw out horizontal shadows like sundials fixed in a time that would never change.

When he stood still he himself became a figure in the rigid landscape. He let his eyes take it in, the verticals measured and spaced by shadow lines, the jetty edge a tall step above the smooth black floor of the water in which the twin globes lay reflected. It was like a painting. The air he breathed was not natural air but the everlasting, unexhausted air of a picture, trapped in the threads of the canvas and held in the grains of the paint. Nothing would ever move.

Only his eyes lived. His sight progressed into the picture, like an invisible wanderer. Beyond the row of bollards that spaced out the perspective a solitary derrick threw a single arm at an angle to direct the eye into the shrinking recessions of the landscape beyond the hill. At its base a squat structure blocked one line of sight yet held him for a moment because it was vaguely man-shaped. He played with it, turning it into a companion at the other end of the quay, before allowing it to become once more a piece of machinery, neglected and shrouded, unused for years.

'Young man!'

The voice, like everything else on the picture's surface, was close to him. Yet it had the echoes of distance in it as though it travelled along harsh corridors. It surrounded him, coming from all angles, but he knew he did not have to turn. Its source was somewhere facing him.

He waited. There was no pulse of life in the night and he, like every other object, was held still.

'Young man, we have not yet met.'

No. He rejected it. But the hard syllables came at him again.

'For some time I have sought you.'

Memory stirred, but Bran fought against it. There was no face with the voice.

'So – well met, Mr Fenby.'

He was in the hall at home. His mother and father were behind the closed door. The voice was with them.

Beside the derrick the shape of the shrouded machinery changed. Once more it was a man, short and square-shouldered. A hat brim cast a diagonal shadow across its almost featureless face. An arm came up and the hat was raised an inch.

'We have things to say, Mr Fenby.'

'No !'

Bran heard the metallic ring of his own voice against the silent hill. He shouted again to erase the man, the bringer of ill-luck.

'No !'

'Yes, Mr Fenby.'

The figure took a pace forward. Bran saw only the foot advance to touch the first horizontal shadow. He wrenched himself around and began to run.

He was leaden limbed. The picture clung and would not free him. He heard the desperate scuffle of his feet and the panic of his breath but he did not seem to move.

Fear surged over him, netting him from behind. There could be no escape. He let his pace slow, giving up hope. And then, without seeming to have covered any ground, he saw that he was almost at the lock gate.

He looked back. The weeds of the path had closed behind him. Nothing followed.

25

Stella, a shadow herself, stood on the square mass of darkness made by the lock gate. He could not see her face, but he knew she was watching him and he slowed his pace still further.

The gate flung one of its great wooden arms across the path as though deliberately to guide him towards her and he paused when he reached it, still breathing heavily from running, and rested against it. The heavy beam seemed to thrum with the energy needed to hold back the weight of water.

'You're late.' Her voice filtered down through the dimness.

'Were you waiting for me?' It was the last thing he expected of her and his heart leapt, but his hopes sank when she answered.

'I saw Sandy go by a long time ago,' she said. 'You'll find her in the square with the others.'

'No,' he said. 'I wasn't looking for her.'

'That's up to you.' She began to move away.

'Stella.' She waited as he climbed the two wooden steps that put him level with her. 'I'm sorry about this afternoon.' Her hand rested on the rail and he slid his fingers along until he was almost touching her. 'I mean I'm not sorry. I'm not sorry at all. I'm glad. I wanted it to happen.'

She saw that his hair had gathered what little light there was and showed almost white against the blackness of the trees. She longed to surrender to him as he had done to her. But he knew so little; nothing at all of the bargain that had made her spy on him and Sandy together. She opened her mouth to tell him but Harman's yellow glare suddenly filled all her mind and she shrank from revealing to Bran how deeply she had betrayed him. He was stooping slightly in order to be nearer her and the warmth of his hand seemed to reach her along the rail. All she need do was remain still and he would come to her.

Then she was saying, 'Did I hear you running?' and her fingers began to curl under her palm away from him.

'Perhaps.'

He did not seem to have heard her. She clenched her fist and drew it away from the rail. 'Because somebody *was* running.'

He straightened. 'It must have been me.'

'Why?'

'I felt like it.' Instinctively he shied away from the real reason and then spoke lightly, trying to disguise it even further. 'I must have known you were waiting for me.'

It was a false note and they both recognized it. He glanced back along the shrouded path but shadows had closed in on it as securely as if a gate had been shut, and nothing moved. She turned away from him slowly.

'I'm going into the village,' she said.

'We'll go together.'

'They'll say things.'

'I don't care.'

Her step hesitated and he almost ran into her. She spoke to him over her shoulder.

'And there's Griff.'

He was cautious. 'Yes,' he said, 'there's Griff.'

'I know you're not afraid of him.'

'I could be.'

'I'm not thinking about you. I don't want to see him humiliated.'

'You needn't worry, Stella. There'll be no more of last night. That's finished as far as I'm concerned.'

'That's not what I'm talking about. I mean he must not think that just because of what happened I don't want him.'

'Do you?'

There was no glint of life, of any sort of understanding, in the dark cavities of her eyes, and she gave no answer.

'Very well,' he said, and he allowed distance to expand between them as they passed through the alleyway and out into the square.

Laughter surprised him. It came from the grove. People were moving among the trees that, seen from the other side of the water, had seemed only minutes before to be deserted.

He hung back slightly so that, unseen by her, he could look beyond the grove to the end of the square where the lamps formed a bright gateway to the dark hill beyond. Under its looming mass the jetty made a grey line on which the bollards squatted like motionless dwarfs. He saw the derrick's crooked arm, but the shape that had been beneath it had disappeared.

Then Sandy's voice, with a shriek of laughter. 'Griff! Don't do that!'

He saw the two figures struggling and his mind lurched. Time had twisted back on itself in a transparent fold, laying event on event, endlessly repeating. There could be no escape.

'You'd better stop.' Sandy was loud, enjoying

herself. Griff had an arm around her and seemed about to pick her up. 'Don't you dare. You remember what happened last time.'

'He don't worry me.'

'He would if he was here.'

Griff stooped swiftly and took her off her feet. 'Tell him,' he said. 'Send somebody to fetch him.'

He began to spin with her but suddenly she tugged at his shoulder, making him stop, and for the second time in two nights he and Bran faced each other across the arena.

'Hello, Bran.' Sandy spoke sweetly. 'We were just talking about you, weren't we, Griff?'

The big man began to lower her.

'No,' she said, 'there's no need to put me down. He's brought his own company, can't you see?'

'We only met by chance,' said Stella. 'He was looking for you.'

'I'm sure.' Her feet were released and swung to the ground. 'Oh well,' she looked up at Griff, 'if you must. But I didn't hear him tell you.'

Griff's voice was a thin, menacing wheeze. 'He don't worry me. I told you.'

'Of course not. What happened last night could never happen again. I know that. He told me himself it was just a lucky punch.' She turned to look at Bran. 'You wouldn't like to have to do it again, would you?'

Bran knew what must happen next. He did not reply.

Sandy lowered her eyes and spoke softly, but loud enough for everybody within the grove to hear. 'You wouldn't dare.'

Bran began to move, caught within the repeating tide but knowing that this time the outcome would be different. He had gone no more than half a step when Stella caught at his arm, pulling him back.

'Don't listen to her! She's doing it deliberately.'

He began to disengage himself, saying nothing.

'She wants to see you hurt. Can't you see that?'

Sandy laughed, showing her anger. 'And why should I do that, Stella?'

'Because you are what you are.'

'And you – what are you?' Sandy's anger burst. She swung towards Griff. 'You know where they were this morning, these two? At the top of the hill. They had a meeting up there that you didn't know about and nor did I.'

'It was an accident,' said Bran.

'Some accident!'

Stella said, 'I was already there, watching the sunrise. I didn't tell anybody; nobody knew.'

'Typical.' Sandy was scornful. 'Never letting anybody know anything. Full of secrets.'

'Not at all like you.' Stella's voice was barely audible. 'You have no secrets, of course.'

'What do you mean by that?'

'Nothing.' Stella glanced sideways and Bran saw that she was appealing for help. She did not want to be pressed, but Sandy was aware of it and did not relent.

'Come on, Stella, tell me what it is I'm keeping secret.'

The whole grove fell silent, awaiting Stella's reply. Bran did not know how to help.

'Well?' said Sandy.

Stella suddenly raised her face and shook her hair back. 'You keep hinting at things you've got that nobody else is supposed to know about; only you.'

'What sort of things?'

Stella shrugged, not wanting to answer, and suddenly Bran realized what was in her mind.

'Potter Waterfall's box,' he said.

'That's nothing to do with her.'

'Well it is something to do with me.'

'So you've told her, I suppose. Something that was entirely private, in our family for years and years, then you come along, and without a word to anybody else, you tell her!' Sandy's lip curled.

Bran began to answer, but Stella's voice overrode him.

'He told me nothing. I found out for myself. I know what you hide under the sundial.'

'He must have told you that.'

'No.'

'Then how do you know?'

Her glance flickered towards Bran and he drew in his breath, ready to answer for her but she shook her head slightly. She even seemed to smile before her eyes moved back towards Sandy.

'I moved the sundial myself. Nobody else was there.'

'You sneaked into my house?' Sandy was aghast.

Stella nodded.

'Like a thief? Like a burglar?' Sandy's sense of outrage grew. 'You broke into my house!' She was a wronged, provoked housewife, summoning up generations of correct behaviour. 'Have you ever heard the like!'

Only a moment before, she had been squirming in Griff's arms, a temptress, and now this hypocrisy. Bran found himself speaking.

'You caused it,' he said. 'You let her know half of the secret and deliberately kept her out of the rest. I don't blame her for finding out. That's all she did. She wasn't there to steal, and you know it.'

Sandy swung towards him.

'Yes, you stand up for her. She's one of your sort: sneaky, dishonest.'

By an effort he kept his voice level. 'She's no worse than you, Sandy. We're all about the same.'

Her lips were very thin and her nose was pinched and white. 'I am not the same as her! You might be. You probably are as you come from the same sort of background. Horrible little people in horrible little houses!'

Her cruelty affected even Griff. He tried to hold her hand and draw her back, but she shook him off.

'No!' She was almost shouting. 'She thinks she's in the know. Well she isn't. She knows about the box and what's in it but there's still something else. Something that she can do nothing about because she's an outsider.' She drew in her breath. 'And I can prove it!'

26

'Wait there!'

Sandy's order was shouted over her shoulder and she was out of the grove and walking across the square before anybody stirred.

The group among the trees found themselves scattered, without a centre, and began to shift about awkwardly, not knowing at which point to gather. Tentative moves were made towards Stella but she kept herself at the outskirts, shifting until she had shed everybody but Bran, and the rest gradually congregated around the large figure of Griff. Bran looked towards him and made up his mind. He began to move away from Stella towards the group.

'Where are you going?' Her voice was already behind him.

'I want to speak to him.'

'Wait!'

But he was already at the edges of the group and they were letting him through. He did not pause until he and Griff faced each other. The silence around them held everything still, and once again Bran found himself outside what was happening and looking in on a ritual that he wanted no part of but which had to play itself out.

'So it's not over yet.' He was surprised how steady his voice held, but the words brought no response. 'She has something in store for us.'

Still nothing from the face heavily barred with shadow. The big man was wary and menacing. He was being put to the test again and knew it.

'Can I ask you something?' said Bran.

Griff's shrug was barely perceptible.

'Are you afraid of me?'

The silence crept into a new dimension. Bran stood within two paces of Griff, his arms by his sides. The heavy shoulders in front of him seemed to rise as the head dipped, and then the fists came up slowly. Still Bran stood. The boxer inched forward and suddenly his left shot out. A moaning gasp came from the watchers, but there was no sound of bone on bone. The fist had stopped alongside Bran's cheek and stayed there.

The pause stretched a long second and then came Griff's wheeze. 'Afraid of you, mate?' The fist by Bran's cheek uncurled and the big hand patted his face. He could see Griff's self-confident grin.

Bran allowed himself to be patted once more and then said, 'Well that seems to answer that.' The laughter of relief came from all around them and Bran waited until it had almost subsided before he spoke again. 'I'd rather have you for me than against me – any day.'

Griff lowered his hands and stood back. It was possible to tell from the way he held himself that honour had been restored, and Bran, content, turned away and allowed himself to be outside the group again, moving towards where Stella was still aloof.

He expected her to say something but she was silent and motionless. He looked closer in the dim light and could just see the glint of a tear as it ran down her cheek.

'This morning,' he said, 'when you were ironing and

you didn't know we were watching.' He paused and then went on. 'You were beautiful. Against the white wall,' he said. 'I saw what you are like.' He remembered the way her eyelashes lay along her cheeks as she read, the outline of her slightly parted lips. 'And you are beautiful.'

She dipped her head. 'Leave me alone. You don't know me.'

'Well enough.' He reached for her but she moved back.

'You're better off with Sandy,' she said.

'Everything's changed,' he said. 'You know it has.'

'At least she's honest.' Stella stood back. 'I'd only betray you. Don't trust me.'

He was about to reply when he saw beyond her that Sandy was on her way back.

She swept past them barely bothering to look, and they followed her as the others jostled forward to stop near the stone trough. She had been up to the house and was carrying the box. Questions about it crowded in on her but she ignored them all and put it down on the trough's broad edge. She made them stand back.

'Nobody touch it,' she ordered. 'It's very valuable.'

'It looks old,' said a girl.

'It's a family heirloom.' Sandy's eye caught Bran's and he saw her switch suddenly from taking credit for the box to denigrating it because it belonged to him. 'But it's not the box itself. It's what it contains that's important.'

He shrugged, letting her have her way, but suddenly, at his side, Stella was speaking. 'The box is a lot more valuable than anything inside it.'

Sandy was caught unawares and was angry. 'How do you know?'

'I've been told how much the box is worth.'

'Who? Who told you?'

'Somebody who knows.'

Bran tried to see into Stella's face but she deliberately kept her head turned so that only her profile was visible.

'Well it so happens,' Sandy was triumphant, 'you're wrong. What it contains may not look much but, for anybody who knows about it, it's worth a thousand times more than the box.'

Bran came to Stella's aid. 'All that's in it is a recipe for a pottery glaze. Nothing of great value.'

'My cousin,' Sandy spoke sarcastically as she opened the lid, 'is doing his best to confuse you. He knows very well it isn't just a glaze for a lot of old pots. And so do I. And so does my mother.'

'But your father discovered it was the glaze,' he said. 'That's what he believes it is. And so do I.'

'Then why is he always talking to you about something else?'

She did not want him to say what it was, and he took pleasure in revealing it.

'Alchemy,' he said.

'Yes, that.'

'Turning base metal into gold.' He elaborated for the sake of the others, and also because it was against her wishes. 'Potter Waterfall was an alchemist. There are some people who might think that what's in that box could turn things into gold.'

'Gold?' said somebody. 'Are you serious?'

'No,' he said. 'It's a glaze.'

'All I know,' Sandy spoke directly to him, ignoring the others, 'and you know it as well, is that there's something strange about it.'

She lifted out the phial but too many shadows fell on it for the others to see what it was, so she pushed through them to the patch of light under the centre globes and waited until they had once more gathered around her. She held up the pottery flask, supporting it only by the pressure of a finger at each end. Somebody reached for it.

'Don't touch!' Then she looked directly at Bran. 'I don't want him saying anybody had anything to do with it except himself.'

She let her free fingers curl around so that they just touched the side of the flask and, as they came into contact, she let him see the little spasm that crossed her eyes. She meant him to know that she felt heat from the fluid within and that Stella, an outsider, could never ever detect it.

'Here you are.' She reached towards him. 'You hand it to her.'

He let her place the little flask on his palm. It was a ridiculous test. She had willed herself into a state when she believed in a family magic, a superiority unattainable by those not of the blood. She deluded herself. There was no heat within the clay. It lay quite cold upon his hand.

'This is stupidity,' he said.

'Don't give her any clues!'

'There's not the effect you expect.' He let his finger begin to trace the lines incised in the flask's surface. And suddenly, beyond all expectation, the tip of his finger within the groove was bitten by fire as sharp as a needle. He held himself rigid. Yet she had seen. Her eyes gleamed at him. She knew.

Slowly he withdrew his eyes from hers. Nobody else had seen what passed between them. The moment had been too concentrated and intimate. He turned.

'Stella,' he said.

She put out her hand. Very slowly, as though they

were both at the centre of some ceremony that had just reached its climax, he lowered the flask on to her palm. Only he saw what happened next. Around them, grasses blown by a sudden gust, the heads of all the others turned to face the same direction as something happened at the edge of the grove. His gaze alone was steady and none but he saw Stella flinch. As the pottery touched her skin a dart of pain shot through her. He saw it in her face and felt her hand tremble. But she held his eyes and forced her fingers to curl around the flask.

'You know what it is,' he murmured.

She nodded. 'Heat,' she said. 'Heat inside it.'

His heart leapt. Sandy had no triumph over her. He took the flask from Stella and turned to Sandy. But she had seen nothing. Her attention, like that of all the others, had been dragged away. He followed the direction of their gaze.

A stretch of dusty earth lay between them and the stone trough, and behind it the darkness had gathered and become solid. Solid enough to form a shape.

Nobody moved, but for Bran the whole night seemed to revolve on a vast turntable. The figure he had run from on the quayside faced him again. And on the edge of the trough, out of reach, its lid flung open, the box gaped.

27

Harman stood motionless, and his presence grew outwards like a crystal through the grainy night until it touched them. Only then, when he held each one of them, did he raise his hat. The movement was precise but slightly jerky, like a mechanical figure on a clock, repeating itself for Bran. He waited, as if for the arm to fall clumsily and mark the hour, and once again there came the voice he had heard in the corridor long ago.

'We are fated, Mr Fenby.'

The corridor was grey and endless and there was no escaping it. 'Yes,' he said.

'We have matters to discuss.'

Bran made no reply. He was aware of the others rustling around him, but they were as insubstantial as the village beyond the grove. Everything that had happened, all that he had ever known, was suddenly, terrifyingly, telescoped. Event piled upon event, flicking down like transparent pages, each separate, yet, as they fell upon each other, condensing to a single core, a tiny bead that held every experience in bright, intense miniature. Time ceased there; motion became motionless and opposites combined. Sadness flooded into joy and made it complete.

'So if you will approach, Mr Fenby.'

The bead dwindled to a point and vanished. On the edge of the trough the little box, like a gaping toad, was within arm's length of the man who desired it above all else. The present moment had still to be faced. Bran moved forward across the dusty earth, aware that he was towing the others with him. He heard the shuffling of their feet but saw only the grey shape with the band of darkness thrown by the hat brim.

He stopped when he himself was within reach of the box and searched the shadowed face for the eyes but saw only the crevices through which they were focused on him.

'We have many witnesses, Mr Fenby.' The thin line of the mouth expanded slightly, smiling. 'Yet our business is private.'

'Not now. And there is nothing to be said.'

For reply Harman tilted his head, just enough for the eyes to pick up light. They became twin sparks of malevolent pale fire, and Bran felt the chill of fear. And more. His will was being sucked away, emptied by the force that was turned on him. He was alone, in an empty corridor, and had to do what he was bidden.

'It is a question of unfinished business, Mr Fenby.' Bran heard the voice echo in his head. Nothing else existed. 'A matter that began with your mother and father.'

Bran was again outside the room where they had talked to this man. The door was closed and he would never now be able to open it. The sickening hollowness saved him. Trying to shut out the misery, he closed his eyes.

'Mr Fenby!'

The order was sharp but Bran's mind was elsewhere. He kept his eyes closed.

The voice came again, but softened, attempting to be persuasive. 'Your parents were people of great charm. And honesty. Their son must surely be the same.'

Bran heard his own voice reply. 'She wouldn't sell to you. You couldn't make her.' And it was true; Harman had not been able to undo the generations of determination to keep the box in one family; only her love for Bran and his father had made her decide to relinquish the box. And she had died.

'Look at me, Mr Fenby.'

Bran's eyelids trembled. He was about to obey, but he hesitated, flinching from the power of the man, and for the second time he was saved. He knew, suddenly, that he must not meet those eyes.

Bran began to turn away, clenching his fists, and as he did so he became aware of what he gripped. Slowly he uncurled his fingers and the possibility of triumph began to trickle in his blood. This was something Harman knew nothing about. Bran, careful not to raise his eyes, advanced his hand to show the phial lying across his palm like a brown slug.

Harman seemed barely interested. He would not be deterred by a ploy like this.

'You have not seen this,' said Bran.

Harman remained still, waiting for the distraction to evaporate.

'You did not even know it existed when you came for the box.'

The man was immovable.

'But it belongs with it.' At last Bran's words brought the faintest twitch of attention. 'The box was made to hold it.'

'Do not joke with me.' All the harshness that had been hidden came out.

'They say it is the secret of the green glaze,' said Bran. 'But not everybody believes that.'

He paused and the silence stretched until impatience overcame the man.

'What, then!' Anger stiffened the shape in the grey, smooth suit but Bran turned away to look at Sandy. Her eyes tried to meet his but were continually trembling away, drawn back to Harman. Face to face with him, without her parents, her confidence was dwindling.

'Well?' Bran asked her. 'Do I say?'

She managed to shake her head. 'Nobody's supposed to know,' she whispered.

'Yes,' said Bran. He reached forward and, taking great care, lowered the flask into the box. He heard the faint sound it made as it rolled into its hollow, and let his fingertips linger in the grooves. There may or may not have been heat there; it was impossible to tell whether he had deluded himself. But to Harman he said, 'I'm sorry. I am not allowed to tell you.'

He was closing the lid when, so swiftly that Bran was unaware of the movement, Harman had reached across the corner of the trough to grip his hand. It was a handclasp, as though they had struck some bargain, and beneath it the lid fell shut.

'You will please tell me, Mr Fenby, what it contains.'

Bran shook his head. He attempted to withdraw his hand, but the pressure was gauged just enough to prevent him. Harman's fingers were hard and dry, inhuman.

'It is, as it happens, an academic question.' Bran was aware, from the corner of his eye, that the mouth smiled, satisfied. 'And as I am aware of Silas Waterfall's other interests, I can hazard a guess – an alchemical guess – at what it is supposed to contain.'

He waited for a response, and when none came, he

176

said to Bran, 'In any case I can study it at my leisure, because I am here – as you must know, Mr Fenby – to collect what is rightfully mine.'

'Not the flask!' Sandy cried. 'That's mine!'

Harman's head inclined a fraction. 'It is open to negotiation, young lady. I am here because I made an agreement with Mr Fenby's parents, and they would expect him to honour it.'

'There is no agreement,' said Bran.

The others saw his shoulders twist as Harman's grip bit into his bones.

'But there *is* an agreement.' The harshness of the voice took on a sharper edge. 'I have your hand on it.'

The pain burned from the twisting bones in Bran's hand to his elbow.

'No,' he said, but the sound that came from him was more like a gasp.

'I think you must say yes.'

Bran's whole arm and side were caught in a flood of anguish. He twisted away but there was no release. His mouth opened and as he fought to prevent a whimper escaping he did not see Griff separate himself from the rest. But he heard the thin wheeze of his voice.

'Let go, Harman.'

Bran brought his head round, moving it against a weight of pain. Griff's round face was a yard from him. Again the voice.

'Want any help?'

He nodded, grimacing.

'Good. I got a debt to pay.'

Griff began to move, circling behind the man, but with a sudden backward lunge Harman heaved Bran around the end of the trough and out of arm's reach. For a fraction of a second during the move the pain eased and Bran wrenched to free himself, but uselessly. Harman was once again planted squarely in front of him and his arm was locked in a pain that went through him to the ground. But with it came a flicker of hope.

'Tell him,' said Harman, 'to keep his distance.'

Bran gambled. He shook his head and just before the pain shut his eyes he saw what he had hoped. Griff stepped forward, and as he did so Harman leapt backwards. The movement was too brief and his muscles too numb to resist, but now he knew what must be done.

'Tell him.' Harman's voice seemed like the edge of pain itself.

Bran let his head loll, mouth open. 'Griff.' He let his voice weaken so it was barely audible. 'Listen.' Griff was allowed to advance half a step. 'Do just as I say.'

'Yes, mate.'

'Tell him to keep back!' Harman ordered.

The pressure increased and Bran no longer resisted. He sank to the ground, kneeling at Harman's feet. He gasped, breathing deep, and suddenly yelled, 'Get behind his back! Lift him! Get him off the ground.'

A bone somewhere in his hand gave. He heard the small, brittle crack but it seemed far off and he was almost indifferent to it. He saw Griff pounce, beautifully smooth. His arms went around Harman, pinioned his elbows to his sides, and in the same movement Griff leaned backwards and the squat, grey man was lifted. Bran saw his hand slide free, felt it jar as it swung to his side. With his other hand he pushed himself to his feet and stood back.

'Hold him there,' he said. 'Clear of the ground.'

Harman was stiff, helpless in the circle of Griff's

arms, and Bran knew that what he suspected when Harman leapt backwards was true. Out of contact with the ground, as though he drew power from it like some charged fluid, he was without strength.

Bran advanced. The danger was now Griff's, but Griff did not realize it. He spun round with Harman and called out, 'Now who's master!' He began to walk away, outside the grove, and Bran followed. 'Shall I drop him in the canal for you?' he called.

But the voice that answered him was Stella's. 'You can put him down,' she said. 'I have what he wants.' She had the box in her hands, and as they watched her she stepped back clear of the group. 'He will do nothing while I have this,' she said.

Griff turned his head, seeking advice.

Bran said, 'Do what she says.'

Slowly, reluctantly, Griff lowered Harman's feet to the ground and stood away from him.

'Step well back,' Stella ordered. 'Let him go free.'

Both Bran and Griff gave the man space. Harman, with the slightest of movements, smoothed his clothes and walked away from them. They expected him to leave the grove completely, depart defeated, but he stopped when he had reached the other side of the trough, with Stella some distance beyond him. Then he turned and spoke.

'You have done well to obey the young lady,' he said. 'We can now all go our ways.'

'You certainly can go,' Griff called to him. 'We want no more of you.'

One of the triple globes in the tops of the trees threw down light that was reflected from the trough into Harman's face. Even at a distance they could see it flicker in the eyes that had been turned back towards Stella and were now levelled at Griff.

'You seem to lack understanding of what has just occurred,' he said. 'The young lady is my associate. And has been for some time. The box is now with us.'

28

Bran watched without believing. Harman was moving with his strange, gliding walk towards Stella and she, her eyes fixed on his, stood still, awaiting him.

Bran refused to let it be true. But then, like a sickness, her words rose in him: do not trust me. The sharp pain that ran from hand to shoulder was extinguished: do not trust me. The eyes he had seen brim with tears were bright on Harman: do not trust me. She had allowed Bran to touch her and had told him not to give her his trust. Now she waited with the box and Harman had only a few paces to go.

Bran began to run but the distance was too great. 'Stella!'

His cry startled her.

'Stella I do trust you!'

She drew back a step. She seemed dazed, looking from him to Harman and back again.

'Go!' he shouted. 'Go! I shall find you!'

She stumbled back, bewildered, seeming half in a dream, but the box was out of Harman's reach and Bran was thudding nearer. The man spun to meet the threat behind him, arms spread. Bran, going too fast to stop, was within range of the short, stabbing arms when a blow in his back sent him sprawling. He fell on his damaged hand and anguish obliterated everything.

Then he was rolling in the dust with Griff, and Griff

was lurching to his feet, hauling Bran with him. 'Saved you again, mate,' said the thin, choking voice.

Harman was no longer concerned with them. He had left the grove, but far beyond him a girl was running.

'She got away,' said Bran. He was nursing his hand, screwing up his eyes.

'That's Sandy,' said Griff.

'Where's Stella?'

'Gone. A long way off. Safe at home by now, I expect.'

Harman, outpaced, seemed to give up the chase. He swung his broad shoulders like a bull about to attack anything that came near. Griff was about to taunt him when Bran, with his good hand, turned him away. 'Don't even look at him!' He dragged Griff away, circling the spot where Harman stood, until they were beyond him and heading towards the corner of the square where Sandy had disappeared.

'I don't want those two girls to meet,' said Bran.

'You're right.' Griff's voice was troubled. 'Sandy's wild.'

'Think you can control her?'

They had begun to run, but the round face turned towards him. 'You want me to try?'

'You'd be better than me.'

'Mean that?' Griff almost halted.

'Of course I do.'

And neither of them needed to say more. Both knew what had happened and who Sandy would now choose.

In the dim alleyway they slowed, and Bran followed Griff on to the lock gate. There was a glimpse of Sandy ahead, but Griff swore. She had seen them and had redoubled her pace. They ran, but they were still only halfway across the water when they heard the gate of the lock-keeper's cottage slam behind her.

They paused in the path outside and then lifted the latch and ventured in. They walked silently between the beds of flowers and around the end of the house. They could hear voices. They stopped moving and listened. There was a man's voice.

'Thank God,' said Griff. 'Her father's there. They won't say much in front of him.'

They listened again but the words were inaudible. And the conversation was brief. A door closed and Sandy came bursting round the corner.

'She's not there!' Anger had not left her voice. 'Her father's not seen her. But she came this way. I know she did.'

Griff tried to say something but she pushed him away. 'I've got to go home,' she said. 'I've got to tell them. I've got to tell my father.'

She went swiftly along the path and was soon within the gloom of the trees.

They hurried and were close behind her when they went through the gate and climbed the garden steps. There were lights in one downstairs room, at the front, but the rest of the house was in darkness. They crossed the lawn, moving almost silently towards the lightless side of the house, and had almost reached the path leading to the back when they heard footsteps. Sandy, in the lead, flattened herself against the wall and they ranged themselves behind her, keeping their breathing shallow, listening.

The footsteps paused and then came on again, but cautiously, hesitated once more, and then whoever it was stepped out from the shelter of the house into the open.

Sandy lunged before anybody else. They heard a

small, faint cry and then two bodies in a hasty, wordless struggle. Sandy straightened.

'I knew it!' Sandy held Stella by the arm. 'I knew it was her!'

Stella, with her free hand brushed the hair from the side of her face. She looked at none of them.

'Where is it!' cried Sandy. 'The box!'

'Where it belongs.' Stella spoke softly.

'You've hidden it where he can find it.' Sandy was shaking her. 'Where is it?'

'She knows where it came from.' Bran stepped forward and reached to separate them, wincing at the stab in his hand. 'That's where she's put it.'

'And you believe her? After all she's done?'

'I believe her.'

'We can soon find out.'

Sandy was breathing heavily. There was still a risk that she would do something to hurt the other girl who stood where she was, her shoulders slightly stooped, awaiting whatever happened next.

'Let her go,' said Bran. 'She won't run.'

Sandy thought about it and then released her, flinging Stella's arm away, forcing her to spin round and pushing her ahead of them to the back of the house.

It was Bran who opened the conservatory door and made them enter quietly. If he could prevent it, he would not disturb Sandy's parents and bring extra shame on Stella. He moved stealthily in the gloom across the floor and searched among the leaves of the vine for the switch. The single bulb leapt into light and showed them themselves standing as motionless as garden statues on the flagstones, and, to one side, the sundial.

All seemed as normal – except that, at the base of

the pedestal, there was an extra shadow. The cavity, uncovered, gaped back.

Sandy shot forward and knelt by it.

'It's empty!' she said. 'She's cheated us!' She scrambled to her feet. 'Hold her!'

But Stella, nearer than any of them to the outer door, made no attempt to get away.

'I've not been in here,' she said. 'I didn't move it.'

They gazed at her and believed her. And, as they did so, the same question chilled each of them. Somebody else had been here. In the sickly light their eyes probed the shadows.

He was not even hiding. He stood to one side of the outer door, where they must have passed him as they entered, and now he guarded their way out. They realized their mistake. When they were at Stella's house, Harman had gone by on the path outside.

Now he came forward, the shadows of the leaves moving down and across his body, grey suit, grey hat.

'It was I who moved this pedestal.' He rested his hand on the sundial. 'Having been told of this hiding place by my associate.' He bowed towards Stella. 'To whom I must apologize for doubting her integrity. I had feared that the incident in the village below had weakened her loyalty, and that she had been misguided enough to return the Waterfall relics to their rather insecure hiding place.'

Sandy began to speak, raising her voice almost to a shout. 'You have no right!' She was moving towards the house to fetch her father, but Harman's yellow eyes were on her and gradually her movement slowed.

'Don't look at him!' Bran's warning came too late. Both Griff and Sandy, like terror-stricken, bewildered children, stood in front of him and did not move. Bran turned away, about to run indoors, but the voice at his back was unhurried, unconcerned.

'One moment,' Harman said, and Bran paused. 'You may fetch her parents if you wish, but it will bring neither you nor them any benefit. The box is, to all intents, in my possession, and shall remain so.'

'No.' Stella's voice was very small.

Bran jerked, beginning to spin round, and then stopped. He had a clear view of what was happening in the reflection of the glass wall. Stella was slightly to one side of Harman out of immediate range of his eyes.

'No,' she repeated. 'It is not in your possession. It is in mine.'

'I fail to understand you.' The voice from the grey shape menaced her.

'Listen to me,' said Stella. 'You will leave now, and when you have gone I shall fetch it and return it to its owners. You will never have it.'

Bran watched. Harman did not move – except for the fingers of the hand that rested on the pedestal. They curled around the sundial's jutting spike, the angled gnomom that told a useless time in the false light. Metal grated on stone and the brass plate tilted. It was the one sign of his fury and the power of it brought terror. The hand twisted until the heavy screws tore from the stone. The sundial was lifted clear. Only then, clutching the metal, did he step away from the pedestal.

Bran was too late in realizing his intention. He backed closer to Stella, keeping his eyes on the other two, then suddenly reached out and grabbed her by the arm. The movement took his eyes from them and Sandy opened her mouth to scream, but Harman said, 'No, young lady,' and raised the metal spike to hold it over Stella like a knife.

'Crude,' said Harman, 'but effective. You will not provoke me, I imagine.'

Sandy ignored him and shouted. With the briefest of movements, Harman jabbed downwards and then immediately lifted the spike. On Stella's arm a fat bead of blood swelled and trickled down the bare flesh.

They waited. The night held them with a cold intensity that seemed to throb. But no sound came from the house.

'That is fortunate,' said Harman.

'Her arm.' Bran had spun round, keeping his eye on Stella, and took a step forward but the spike quivered and it was warning enough.

Harman nodded, like a teacher approving, and said, 'Now we shall recover my property. Master Waterfall's footling precautions can no longer keep it from me. There can be no accidents now to come between me and it. I am too close. The young lady will show us where it is.'

'No,' said Stella.

Instantly the point pressed into her cheek, hard enough to have again drawn blood if she had not twisted her head sideways.

'Tell him!' shouted Bran. 'You've got to tell him!'

'More than that, Miss Grey. You must take all of us to it.' Harman forced her head sideways with the point. 'Do you agree?'

She did not answer and as he repeated the question the spike caused her pain.

'Yes,' she whispered. 'It's not in the house.'

'Very well.' He edged her away from the door. 'You will all go ahead of me and not one of you will attempt to raise the alarm.'

Bran's lips and mouth were dry but he spoke. 'You

can't.' His words came out jerkily. 'You can't make it work.'

'The young lady's looks are at stake.'

Bran attempted to speak again but Harman's patience had gone. 'You have underestimated me once. There is no second chance.'

'Stella,' said Bran. 'He can have the box. Tell us where it is.'

'It's out there.' Her voice was muted but still had the break in it, wandering between two tones. 'At the top of the hill.'

At Harman's orders the light was switched off and they went out quietly, Sandy leading, and began to climb the levels of the garden. From time to time Bran looked back, hoping for some sign of life in the house, but it sank away, muffled by the trees, and was submerged.

It was dark in the forest and they stumbled, but every time anyone fell Harman held back and waited until he could pick out each one of them before he let them resume.

When the trees ended they came out into the full face of the moon and stopped.

'Well?' said Harman.

'The hut.'

Smoky cloud lay on the horizon but only the lower edge of the moon was obscured, and in the pools it lay white and almond-shaped as they approached, and vanished as they passed. The moss was soft and the only sound to come from them was their breathing.

They came down to the level where the hut stood.

'The first two will sit down.'

Sandy and Griff had been leading and they sank to the ground. Harman spoke to Stella.

'Now tell the other one where to find it.'

Bran was too far away to see more than the dark hollows of her eyes and the line of her mouth. The man behind her seemed remote, almost part of the landscape.

'Tell me, Stella,' he said.

'Beneath the steps.'

He walked across to where three wooden steps led to the verandah of the hut.

'Here?'

'Yes. Part of it pulls away.'

They were speaking to each other almost as though the others did not exist. He crouched beside the steps.

'Just there,' she said.

The wood was rotten in one place and a board fell away easily. He laid it down and reached inside. He moved slowly and for a moment wondered whether to pretend there was nothing inside, but the risk to her was too great. He reached deeper into the clammy darkness. It was like putting his hand into a grave. Then he felt the ridges of the little casket and lifted it.

'Bring it here!' Harman's voice echoed and died on the wide ledges.

Bran advanced with the box held in both hands.

'Stop. Put it at your feet.'

There was a patch of bare rock five yards from Harman. Bran began to stoop when Stella said, 'I've got to tell Mr Harman something.'

Bran paused, but Harman once again ordered him. 'At your feet. Put it down.'

'Wait!' Stella's cry was full of fear. 'It's important!'

She won a gap. Harman made no move.

'I know the secret, Mr Harman. I know he's got to be careful how he puts that box down.'

'Secret?' Harman's suspicions grew.

'I know about the flask. The heat. I felt the heat.'

But now she was speaking to Bran, gabbling, repeating herself, almost hysterical.

'Sandy thought I'd know nothing about it. But I did. And so did you, Bran. Both of us. Be careful – we know how hot it is.'

She was leaning forward and he was listening.

'And there's the inscription. IN TIME OF NEED. Don't forget.'

And suddenly he saw that her hysteria was faked. She was telling him something.

'The heat, Bran,' she said. 'IN TIME OF NEED.'

The message was too plain. Harman hauled her back savagely. 'Put down that box!'

And Bran had to obey. He leant forward, crouching, in full view, but as he did so he was shifting his hands under the lip of the lid.

The box touched the rock. Now. He pressed upwards with his thumbs, hard, levering the lid up and back. It was flung open and his hand was inside, snatching at the phial. He grasped it and twisted it down with all his strength against the base. He felt its neck fracture. Thick fluid oozed from it. No burning heat.

Harman's shout was loud. 'Stand back!'

The movement had been slight. It could have looked like an accident. Bran shut the lid and got to his feet.

Nothing had happened. The contents of the phial, the supposed Alcahest, was running over the supposed Philosopher's Stone, a cold glaze over a pottery tile, nothing more.

'Sorry, Stella,' he said.

'Back!'

Harman's command rang out and he advanced, still holding Stella, as Bran fell back in front of him.

And between them the box squatted in the pale wash of the moonlight.

Harman was within two paces of it when it vanished. A grey haze enveloped it. A second later the haze broadened, spreading across the moss, and in the centre of it the box still crouched, smoke pouring from under the lid. Then a flicker of flame, a bright sunburst on the rock and a surge of heat.

Bran fell backwards, but in the middle of the flame the figure of Harman lunged and stabbed into the mass of fire with the gnomon, his dagger, seeking to fling out of danger at least the shells of box and flask.

The core suddenly burned white and Harman was caught in it, wrapped in a twisting sheet of flame. He straightened then, at the heart of a roaring column of gases, and sought to escape. But the sheet of incandescence clung, scouring him. Patches of his suit burned into red, glowing threads that whitened and vanished, and he was a scarecrow pushing at a wall of fire. And mouthing. Before the flesh left his face his eyes blazed yellow in one last, blind, random glare that turned up into his skull and vanished.

His slow fall was balanced by the gradual lifting of the roaring column. It shot higher into the night sky, devouring itself until it was a booming flare in the rocking air, howling into a final spiral of red that spun into a thread and vanished above the crumpled black mass that lay on the steps.

Sandy was kneeling in a rock pool and Griff was helping her to her feet. She was whimpering and he was murmuring to her. Above them was the sound of people scrambling down from level to level. It would be her mother and father, drawn by the sudden glare in the sky.

In the glimmer of starlight Stella's face was pale.

Bran put out a hand and her touch was so gentle it was as though she knew of his wound. Both had been marked.

Not far from the blackened heap, near the ashes of the box, there was a glint of metal. Bran kicked it clear. It was the sundial.

'Gold?' he said.

'Maybe. I don't care.'

'Nor do I.'

He picked it up, expecting it to be hot, but it was no more than warm. He held it a moment and then, on the impulse, turned and hurled it out towards the edge of the steps. They heard it strike rock once and then it bounded off into space.

Many years later, and far away, they told their children of the story and there was no rest for them until they returned to the village and made a search below the cliff. There was great excitement when the dial was found, thickly tarnished, wedged between two rocks. Gold? the children asked. Stella and Bran smiled. Gold did not tarnish.